The characters and events portrayed in this book are fictitious. Any similarity to real persons, living or dead, is coincidental and not intended by the author. Any reference to real locations is only for atmospheric effect, and in no way truly represents those locations.

Copyright © 2023 by Ryan Casey

Cover design by Miblart

All rights reserved.

No part of this book may be reproduced in any form or by any electronic or mechanical means, including information storage and retrieval systems, without written permission from the author, except for the use of brief quotations in a book review.

Published by Higher Bank Books

BATTLE FOR SANCTUARY

A Post Apocalyptic Zombie Thriller

THE INFECTED CHRONICLES
BOOK 6

RYAN CASEY

GET A POST APOCALYPTIC NOVEL FOR FREE

To instantly receive an exclusive post apocalyptic novel totally free, sign up for Ryan Casey's author newsletter at: ryancaseybooks.com/fanclub

EMILY

* * *

Emily didn't know what it was like to see until the light came rushing in for the very first time.

She didn't understand it at first. She lived through sounds. She lived through touch. She lived through taste, and she lived through smell.

So when her world opened up with colour, she didn't understand it. She thought it was Heaven. Heaven, and that she'd died, and everything would be okay now.

But the more time passed, the more Emily began to realise it was something very different entirely.

She'd been walking on the road for a long time. Or rather, Dad had been carrying her. A long way. He kept on telling her she was going to be okay. That everything was going to be okay. But that was hard to believe when she could hear the horrible cries they were making. The monsters, as Dad called them. She wished he'd never called them monsters. Because when he called them monsters, Emily couldn't help thinking of the sound of those growls she heard on the horrible films Dad watched. Or the feel of someone's big, hairy hands grabbing her and dragging her away from Dad.

She loved Dad so much. Dad had always been there for her. And Trisha, Dad's new wife, she was nice too, until... well, she didn't want to think about what Trisha did to her. Because it didn't make sense. And it scared her. She didn't want to think about the pain in her shoulder. The *bite* pain in her shoulder.

She just wanted to forget it all.

She thought about Mum. Mum was nice too until she got sick and died. It was a quick illness. One day, they were all out as a family on a walk at the beach. She could hear the sound of laughter. She could smell the salt in the air and the fresh fish and chips, making her hungry. And she could feel the nice cool breeze against her face, and she couldn't wait for the water to touch her toes.

But then she remembered hearing this thump. This bang. This sound of something slapping against the ground. And then a load of gasps nearby, and then...

Dad.

"Lauren!"

Lauren. That was Mum's name. He never usually called her Lauren. He always called her "chick." He only called her Lauren when they were arguing or when he had bad news for her, or when something bad was happening.

The sound of something hitting the ground.

The gasp of people nearby.

And the panic in Dad's voice.

Emily knew right away something was wrong.

Mum had collapsed, apparently. She'd fainted. Only it wasn't just a normal faint. It was a seizure. And a really bad one. And it made her sleep. Made her unconscious. The doctors were worried she wasn't going to wake up from it. Apparently, she had a bleed on the brain, and they were struggling to stop the bleed.

Emily wondered why they couldn't just put a plaster on her

brain like they did with other parts of the body. Plasters always stopped the bleeding whenever she cut herself, whenever she grazed her knees or stepped on sharp things.

She remembered sitting at the side of Mum's bed. She remembered holding her hand. Her hand felt cold. Not warm like it used to feel when she was tucking her in bed or stroking her hair while she told her a story.

Ice cold.

And it made her feel so sad. Because she just sat there in that hospital room where the bleeping kept on going off, with that strong smell of medicine in the air, and she just held Mum's hand and waited for her to wake up again. Waited for her fingers to move again. Waited for her to give her a sign that she was still okay. To wake up from her dream.

But she never did.

When Emily got home from school on Wednesday, 14th November, Dad told her they weren't going to see Mum that night. Because Mum wasn't there anymore.

At first, Emily didn't understand. She asked Dad what he was on about and where Mum had gone if she wasn't at the hospital. She thought at first maybe she'd just moved hospital. Because she was sick. So there was no way she could walk anywhere.

But Dad held her shaking hands and told her she'd gone to Heaven. That she wasn't here anymore. She was with the stars now.

Emily never knew what stars looked like. Dad tried telling her. They were beautiful bright dots in the dark sky. They were angels. They were where people went when they died. A peaceful place.

And although it was hard for Emily to imagine stars—she couldn't taste, smell, or hear them, so her frame of reference wasn't quite there—she knew she was looking at the stars the second the light came rushing in, for the first time in her life.

These beautiful bright lights all around her. Vast. So many of them. Stretching off in every direction.

She could've cried.

She might've cried at the beauty of it. At the thought of Mum being up there.

But there was something else.

Another feeling.

A strange feeling. A feeling like her body was too big for her. Like it wasn't quite right.

She looked down and noticed something weird.

She saw this pattern in front of her. These five worms squeezing out of a bigger mass. A fleshy mass.

And based on where they were and what she could feel there, she realised these weird things must be *hands*.

She couldn't explain it. But her hands looked bigger than they felt normally. And they had these little things sprouting from them, too.

Things that felt like...

Hair.

Hairy hands.

Big, hairy hands.

Not *her* hands.

She stood there. What was happening? What was this? She and Dad were walking. They were walking, and then they found this place, and...

It was all so blurry. She couldn't remember. She couldn't think.

But there was this other feeling.

This weird feeling.

Deep in her bones.

Hunger.

She looked across the room, and she saw something sitting there. Something different to everything else.

This figure. This figure with a moving gap, which must be a mouth, with sound coming out. Sound like... a voice.

And she realised, then. She'd never *seen* before. She'd never seen *anything* before.

But this *creature*.

This... *thing*.

It was a man.

She saw a man sitting there. He was tied up. His hands behind his back. And he was looking at her—or whoever she was—like she was a monster.

"Please!" he begged. "Please, no!"

And Emily didn't understand. 'Cause it didn't make sense. Why was this man so scared of her? Why was she in a man's body?

And why did she feel so...

Hungry?

She stood there. Looking at this screaming man. Not sure what to do. Whether to go and tell him everything was okay.

And then she heard something else, deep inside her.

Take him make him join us and then you can join us too you can join us too...

And that voice.

It was so loud.

It made her body shake.

And that voice felt like it was *her* voice, only in her head. It felt like it was her voice. It felt like it was Dad's voice. It felt like it was Trisha's voice.

It felt like it was...

Mum's voice.

The voices of everyone she'd ever trusted.

Go on take him take him help him spare him make him one of us dear one of us...

And even though she felt bad for this screaming, crying man, even though she didn't want to do anything to hurt anyone—she never wanted to do anything to hurt anyone—she felt this voice deep in her bones, and there was only one thing she could do.

She closed her burning eyes.

She stared into the darkness.

Then she opened her eyes and looked up at the stars above.

Or were they just *lights?*

Was this outside, or was this inside?

She couldn't tell.

She didn't know.

All she knew was this was a man.

Even though he was just a mishmash of colours and things she didn't really understand... he was a man.

And she was hungry.

She looked down at him.

Saw him. And then she saw these two things on his head that must be eyes.

And for some reason, when she saw those eyes looking at her... she could tell he was scared.

She could tell he looked afraid.

She stood her ground.

Her heart raced.

The man screamed.

And then she let the voice and the hunger take over her completely, and she ran over to the man, opened her mouth, and sunk her teeth into his hot, sweaty skin.

* * *

Leonard looked on from afar.

He watched the prisoner writhe around.

He watched the blood pour out of his throat.

And then he looked over at the girl, sitting there, tears of blood rolling down her face, from her nostrils, from her eyes.

"See?" Dean said. "Don't you see now?"

Leonard swallowed a lump in his throat as he watched his prisoner succumb to the worst of fates.

He understood.

And he understood well.

He knew what this meant.

He knew exactly what this meant.

"Take her to her cell," Leonard said, thinking of all this could mean for the barracks. Of all the things this could mean for *everyone*.

Because it wasn't just the ability to enter the minds of the infected.

No, it went further than that.

It was the other abilities she had, too.

The other secrets.

And somehow, Leonard got the sense they were only just scratching the surface.

He looked at Dean. Took a long, deep breath.

"Feed her. Monitor her. Make sure she's hydrated. Make sure she's well. But more importantly... make sure she never sets foot away from our barracks. We have ourselves the most important person we've come across since the outbreak started. And we're going to make damned sure we use her to our advantage."

KEIRA

* * *

Keira staggered across the field, holding Nisha in her arms, and wondered how much further she would manage before she collapsed to the grass.

It was getting late. She'd been walking for what felt like forever. Holding Nisha. Holding her in her arms. She tried not to look down at her. Because looking down at her made her realise what a sorry state she was in. Looking down at her made her realise how bad a condition she was in.

Looking down at her made her face the reality—the possibility—that she'd failed her.

Just like she'd failed Dad.

Just like she failed everyone.

The memory of Dad being bitten flooded her mind as she stumbled across the field, Rufus by her side. Sarah was a little behind her, too. This afternoon's events. None of them made sense. All of them were just this jumbled mess. This jumbled mess in her mind: finding Dad's home. Losing Dad's home. Losing Sarah, Nisha, and Rufus. Dad being bitten, and...

The horde.

The infected horde.

A crowd of infected unlike any she'd ever seen.

Dad slowly fading.

Raising the knife over him and putting him to sleep.

And then Sarah staggering towards her holding Nisha.

Fuck. Yeah. It was a lot.

She glanced down at the unconscious Nisha. She couldn't help it. Couldn't resist. But when she looked at her, it just reminded her how precarious a situation Nisha was in.

Her eyes were closed. Her face was pale. So pale. Little patches of dried blood oozed from her nostrils and her eyes, trickling down her face. She'd passed out. She'd gone after the horde of infected, according to Sarah, and then she'd had one of her seizures and then passed out.

Only this time, the seizure was stronger than any Sarah had ever seen. In the past, when she'd had one of these seizures, she'd soon woken up. Seemed relatively unaffected by them, all things considered.

But this...

This was different.

And it completely fucking terrified Keira.

She thought about that horde of infected. What Sarah told her. Nisha. She'd stood in front of them, and somehow, that horde just... changed direction.

Was Nisha responsible somehow?

And was that why she was in such a dire state now?

She looked back over her shoulder. Saw Sarah running along with her. And further back, she saw the trees. The trees she'd walked away from. The trees she'd left behind.

The trees she'd left *Dad* behind in.

He always said he wanted to die in nature. That he didn't want to be buried and didn't want to be cremated. So it brought her some peace that she could leave him somewhere nice. Somewhere peaceful. Somewhere scenic.

But the thought that Dad was gone at all. It still didn't seem real. It still didn't make any sense. She still hadn't quite even begun to process it.

Because Dad wasn't supposed to die.

Dad was supposed to be different.

Dad was supposed to be different, wasn't he? Because—because he was her dad. And things were getting better between them. He wasn't supposed to die so mercilessly like that. And if he did die, it would be in sacrifice. It would be protecting her. Protecting other people. Something like that. A hero's death. That's what he deserved.

Because... he *was* a hero.

But his death...

His death was so pointless.

And that shook Keira to her core.

She squeezed her eyes shut as she staggered across this field. She clutched Nisha tight. And she realised there was no reason why Dad should've survived at all while so many other people fell victim to this chaos. Dad wasn't different. Just like Mum wasn't different when she'd died in that car crash right beside Keira all those years ago.

Everyone thought they were the heroes of their own story.

Everyone.

Everyone thought they might be different. Everyone thought they might stand a better chance of surviving. Because believing you might be no different from everyone else—believing your existence really was just pointless—that wasn't easy to digest. That wasn't easy to swallow. And it was destructive. Completely self-destructive.

Everyone thought they were special. No one thought they were going to die pointlessly.

But all Keira's years on the wards had taught her just how misguided a belief that really was.

She looked down at Nisha again. Her eyes closed. Her heart still beating lightly, but for how much longer? How long until she died, too? Because, sure, she might be different. She might be special. She might be able to resist the infected.

But she was still human. Which meant she was still vulnerable.

She was still human.

Which meant that she wasn't immune to the horrors of this world.

She thought of all her hope in the early days of this outbreak three weeks ago.

She thought of the optimism that the government might step in and help. That the police might step in and help. That the military might step in and help, that people might stand together against the infected, and that everything might work out in the end. Because it always did. Right?

But no. It was naive to believe that. And it came from a place of privilege, too, didn't it? Because there were so many other countries across the globe whose citizens lived in horror. In terror. Every single day. She was lucky. Sure, Britain wasn't exactly great, and sure, Preston wasn't exactly the most interesting city in the world.

But it was safe.

It was home.

She loved it for that.

And what she'd give right now for an opportunity to turn back the clock. A chance to go back to her relatively mundane everyday existence.

What she'd give right now for a chance to go back and be able to heal her wounds with Dad before any of this broke out.

"Keira," Sarah gasped. She sounded like she was struggling. Like she was in pain.

Keira turned around. Saw Sarah wasn't moving anymore. She'd stopped. She was wincing. She wasn't one to usually wear her heart on her sleeve. Seemed quite a closed book. The emotion in her voice when she walked up to her, Nisha in her arms, was probably the most broken Keira had ever seen her in their three weeks together.

But right now, she looked in agony.

"I can't keep running," Sarah said.

"But Nisha—"

"We've been running for hours," Sarah said.

"We can't just give up. The landing site. Where we saw the helicopter."

"We've passed it. There's nothing there."

"But there *can't* be nothing there," Keira said. "We didn't see the helicopter fly off again. There has to be someone. There has to be somewhere. There has to be some help. There just has to be."

Sarah stared at her with wide, bloodshot eyes. She held her lower back, wincing, struggling to breathe. It was like she didn't want to say the words she was saying but had no choice. She was in pain. She was struggling. Badly.

But the implications of what she was saying.

The suggestion of her words.

"So what are you saying?" Keira asked. "We just give up on her?"

She expected the usual bullshit response. The usual non-answer. Like a politician. The usual evasiveness. The usual crap.

But, much to her surprise, Sarah did something unexpected.

She answered her.

"I'm saying I don't think we have much choice."

Those words. Like a punch to the gut. Keira felt her eyes stinging. A lump swelled in her throat. She shook her head. "I'm not giving up on her."

Sarah shook her head, too. Her eyes looked bloodshot as well. "I'm sorry," she said. "But I don't see what choice we have. I don't see what more we can do—"

"I'm not giving up on her!" Keira shouted.

Her voice echoed around the field. Suddenly, the sky above felt like it grew a shade darker. And Keira didn't feel alone. She felt like someone was close. Like someone was watching.

Close by.

"I can't give up on her," Keira gasped. "I promised... I promised her dad. I promised my friend. And I promised *my* dad. I can't give up on her."

But as she said the words, a shiver crept right down her spine. A shiver of acknowledgement. Of realisation. Realisation that, as much as she hated to admit it—as much as she hated to agree with Sarah—she was probably right.

And she hated it.

Sarah stumbled up to her, Rufus right beside her. She lifted her hand. Then lowered it. And then lifted it again and placed it on Keira's arm. Like it was the hardest thing in the world. "We're not safe out here. We're exposed. We need to shelter. For the night. And then we can... re-assess. Tomorrow. But you know as well as I do that there's only so far we can keep running like this. I'm sorry."

She turned away, then. Walked around Keira. And Rufus walked along with her, tail wagging, tongue dangling out of his mouth, glancing back at Keira and looking at her with this look of concern. Of curiosity.

Keira looked down at Nisha.

She looked at her pale face.

She looked at her weeping eyelids.

"I'm sorry," Keira said. "I'm so sorry."

And then she turned around, tears blinding her gaze, and she walked with Rufus, with Sarah, clinging to Nisha, every single step.

SARAH

* * *

Sarah stared at Keira, standing there with Nisha in her arms, and she really wished she didn't have to give up.

But she didn't see what other choices they had.

Keira's head was lowered. She was holding Nisha close to her chest. Rain fell from the clouds above, which were getting thicker by the moment.

She used to love the cloudy, rainy days as a child. It meant she wouldn't have to go out. She wouldn't be forced to play stupid, inane games with children she didn't like and who didn't like her. She could just stay in her room with a good book and lose herself in the pages.

She preferred factual reads. Fiction often bored her. She found it hard to suspend her disbelief with most books she read. Especially ones sanctioned for her age group at school. If she were to read any fiction, she certainly wouldn't be opting for Roald Dahl at the age of fourteen. If she were to tackle a fictional work, give her a Haruki Murakami or a Hanya Yanagihara any day. Something more intellectually challenging.

But as she got older, she began associating the rainy days with something far more sinister.

The days when Dean wouldn't let her leave.

No. She couldn't think about that. Not now. Thinking about her time with Dean wasn't productive right now. Especially not when Nisha was in such grave danger. And when Keira, after just losing her father, needed all the support she could get.

She looked at Keira. She hadn't said anything about the loss of her dad. Anything at all.

She knew she was trying to be strong. For Nisha. And Sarah knew she had to be strong for both of them.

She couldn't think about the past. Not right now.

She couldn't think of Dean. Not right now.

But that bitter taste filling her mouth.

That gnawing tension tightening its grip around her stomach.

Those were feelings she wouldn't be able to shake off at the click of a finger.

There were memories embodied within those feelings.

And no matter how hard she tried to resist them, no matter how hard she tried to push them away, they just kept on resurfacing.

And they always would.

She watched Keira turn around, Nisha in her arms. She saw Rufus, the dog, glance up at her, raising his ears, wagging his tail. Why had the dog attached itself to her? She'd never really liked dogs. She found their motives hard to interpret.

But admittedly, she couldn't lie; she quite liked this dog. He was more simplistic than other dogs she'd come across. His motives and his intentions were usually rather obvious and clear. He liked food. He liked strokes. And he liked to run. Made a pleasant change to other dogs—the ones that sometimes snapped when you went to stroke them.

Made a pleasant change to most people, too.

She listened to the wind howling against the trees. There was a cool dampness to the air. And there was still a *smell*, too. A smell hanging in the air. The infected. So many of them had walked on past. They were all walking towards David in a large group. Then, pacing towards Keira. And then...

Well, she could remember it perfectly.

Nisha.

Running over to that crowd.

Standing there.

Shaking.

Blood oozing from her nostrils and out of her ears and her eyes.

And then the infected, turning around, walking away.

It sounded far-fetched. But had *she* done that, somehow? She wasn't sure how that could even be possible. But she'd seen other strange things on the road with this girl.

The deterrence of the infected.

The resistance to the bite.

And the time on the road when the infected military man flew at her and then just... froze.

Like, somehow, he was letting Sarah go.

Did Nisha have something to do with that infected man stopping, even when she was unconscious?

And what about the horde of infected, racing towards Keira and David and then just... turning away?

Was this the evolution?

Was this the next step?

But no. She didn't know this with any certainty. She could be imagining things. She could be projecting her suspicions onto this girl. It was dangerous to jump to lofty conclusions without actually considering the real, legitimate facts.

But...

She knew what she'd seen.

And didn't that make Nisha even more important, after all?

She thought back to her conversation with Keira just now as

the pair stumbled weakly through the grass. The suggestion she'd made. The suggestion she'd made about giving up the search for this supposed helicopter because it was a futile mission. What was the alternative? Giving up on the child? No. Of course not. That's not what she was suggesting, even if that's how Keira saw things in her grief-stricken, shocked state.

But one thing was for sure.

Sarah didn't want to get sloppy. She didn't want Keira to get sloppy. It was getting late. Darkness was approaching. They needed to find a place to rest. And once they did, then—and only then—could they begin to consider the next steps.

The next steps for themselves.

And, more importantly, the next steps for Nisha.

She took a deep breath of the mild, breezy air. Watched Keira stumble along, shaking. And as much pain as she was in—as harsh as those bolts of agony splitting and stretching down the length of her spine actually were, and not getting any better, either—she had to keep going. And she had to offer Keira a hand.

She walked over towards Keira and Nisha and tried to imagine the least selfish thing to suggest right now. "Let me take her."

Keira shook her head. Gripped Nisha even tighter. "I'm not letting her go."

"You've been carrying her long enough. You should—"

"I can't let her go, Sarah. Do you understand? I can't just let her go. I can't just give up on her. I have to keep going. I have to keep trying. I can't just give up on her."

And Sarah heard her words, and she sympathised. Truly. Keira had just lost her father. Sarah remembered losing her father. She was always rather good at convincing herself she wasn't emotionally impacted by the most wounding moments of her life. But Dad's death hadn't been easy by any stretch.

She'd tried to smile. She'd tried to force herself to laugh when she heard the news of him jumping to his death from a railway bridge. Because if she could convince herself to smile, convince herself to laugh, then she could convince herself that everything was okay. That she could be strong. She could be strong, and she could fight through it. Just like she fought through everything.

But she hadn't been able to hold that smile.

She hadn't been able to force that laugh.

And she hadn't been able to stop the tears.

And in the years since, she told herself different stories, sometimes. She told herself he was still out there. She told herself that he was still alive. That he was just working away. Or that they just hadn't spoken for a long time. That they'd just grown apart.

But the truth always caught up with her in the end.

"I'm sorry," Sarah said, looking squarely into Keira's eyes. "I understand how important she is to you. And how important your father was to you."

Keira lowered her head.

"And I understand how it might sound. I know it might sound like I'm being defeatist. Like I'm giving up. But that's not the case. We have to try. Like you said yourself. We have to do everything we can for her. But that includes not acting stupidly. That includes not acting... sub-optimally. And blindly following this lead towards a helicopter that led nowhere, right after myself and Nisha were pursued by savages in military uniforms... that feels rather sub-optimal to me."

Keira looked at her. Squarely at her. And for a moment, Sarah feared the worst. She was going to lambast her. She'd said the wrong thing. She'd been insensitive. She'd got it wrong all over again.

And then something surprising happened.

Keira nodded.

"You're right," she sighed. "I mean, you expressed it in the weirdest fucking way imaginable. 'Sub-optimally'. But you're right."

Sarah nodded back. Wow. She was right. How about that? Maybe her powers of perception were getting better after all.

Honestly, she wasn't really thinking through what she was saying. She was just saying what seemed the right thing to say.

As for 'sub-optimal'... what was so wrong with that?

"It looks like the weather's taking a turn," Sarah said. "We need to find shelter. We need to sleep. We need to eat. Or if we can't do any of those things... we at least need to rest. *You* need to rest."

She saw Keira turning around again. Looking away. Staring off into space. Shaking her head, like she was trying her hardest to resist Sarah's words. Her suggestions. Like she was trying her hardest to maintain a strong front, even after everything she'd been through.

Sarah gulped. And perhaps buoyed by Keira's reassurance that her words so far were the right ones, she found herself stepping forward. Right towards her.

Putting a hand on her shoulder.

"It's... okay. To let it out. If you feel... bad. About what happened. And it's okay to... to talk, too. I know I'm not always the best. With this stuff. But I'm... I guess what I'm trying to say is I'm here."

Keira shook her head. But she couldn't fight the emotion creeping across her face. She couldn't hide the tears flowing down her cheeks right as Sarah permitted her to be vulnerable.

"I just..." Keira started. "I need to stay strong."

"And you need to let me carry Nisha for a while," Sarah said. Even though her body ached like mad.

Keira shook her head. "I can't let her go."

"You're not letting her go. Because I've got her. And I'm right here. For her. For... for you."

Keira looked into Sarah's eyes. She looked at her like a dog, trying to convince its owner not to take it to the vet, even though it needed treatment immediately.

Sarah took a step closer to her. As uncomfortable as this closeness felt. "It's okay. I've got you. And I've got her. It's okay." The words felt unnatural. They felt awkward, leaving her lips.

But she knew they were the right words right now.

Keira opened her mouth.

She looked like she was going to resist. Like she was going to protest. Like she was going to stand her ground once again. And maybe a small part inside Sarah *wanted* her to.

"It's okay," Sarah said. "It's okay."

And then, Keira descended into a mass of tears and handed Nisha right over into Sarah's arms.

"I just miss him," Keira cried. "I'm trying to stay strong. Because I know I need to stay strong. There's no time for weakness. No time for any weakness at all. But I just miss him so, so much."

Sarah held Nisha. Even though the weight of her body put pressure on her spine and filled her body with pain, she held her.

And while she held her, she wrapped an arm around Keira. Pulled her close. Tasted the sweat in her hair and the salty tears streaming down her cheeks.

She let her cry on her shoulder. And she kept her arm around her back. And she pulled her closer.

"It's okay," Sarah said. Her own walls crumbling. "I'm here. I'm... I'm right here."

NISHA

* * *

It was that dream again.
She was in the body of a man. And she was walking. Walking slowly at first. Then, walking quickly. Really quickly. She was in some field somewhere. She didn't know where she was. It felt like somewhere she'd been before, but she wasn't sure she had because she was pretty sure it would've been with Dad if she'd been somewhere like this before. Because Dad was the only person she ever really went anywhere with. And as far as she could remember, she never remembered walking through a random field with him.

She could see flashes in the sky. She could see rain falling. And she could *smell* the badness in the air, so strong now. Only... maybe it's because she was in this man's body, but it didn't smell all that bad anymore.

It smelled like home.

Like she was heading home after a long, long holiday.

A holiday she wanted to get home from.

And the weird thing about this dream? She couldn't remember

how she'd got here. She couldn't even be sure it was a dream. She was never usually sure about dreaming. Usually, when she realised she was dreaming, she woke up right away. Woke up the second she realised she was having a nightmare. Opened her eyes. Sometimes crawled out of bed and climbed into bed with Dad. She'd feel better in Dad's bed. She always felt more comfortable there. She always felt safer there.

But somehow, she just *knew* this was a dream.

And the weirdest thing about it?

It felt so real.

The only reason she thought it must be a dream?

Because she was in someone else's body.

Again.

She walked along through the grass. Her feet were sore. Her neck ached, too. She could taste blood on her lips. But it didn't taste metallic and horrid like it usually did. In a weird way, it tasted... nice.

Like barbecued meat.

And she wanted more of it.

Yes, you do, and that's why you're going to be okay, dear; you're the one they follow, you're the one they worship, you're their future, and you're going to make sure you...

That voice. In her head. Only she could... *hear* it. Like words in her skull.

That voice. Speaking to her.

That voice. A voice that *sounded* like someone else talking in her head.

A voice that seemed so familiar.

And somehow, a voice that she could *understand,* even though she'd never actually heard words before.

Was it *her*?

Was she finally able to think in words now she knew what words sounded like?

But how could she *understand* them?

It didn't make sense.

A bang. A loud bang splitting through the sky. It made her feel terrified at first. Because she didn't know what it was. It wasn't a smell, and it wasn't a taste. And even though she could *feel* the ground shaking, she didn't think it was a feeling, either. Not just a feeling anyway.

Just a Feeling. Feeder. That was the song Dad played to her once. Turned the volume right up and played the song really loud, and...

No.

Just don't think of Dad.

Don't think of Dad. Because it will just make you feel sad again.

And you can't be sad right now.

You need to be strong.

You need to...

Wake up.

But she *felt* awake. Inside this man's body, she felt awake. She was walking somewhere. She didn't know where. But she wasn't alone, either. There were others with her. And when she looked around at them, she realised they were bad people.

And suddenly, the memory raced into her skull.

The memory of when she opened her eyes and she was inside another person. And she was racing towards that bad army man, who was standing over Sarah with a gun.

And she could *see* herself. Her own body. Nisha. Lying there. On the ground. Beside Sarah.

It felt so real right then. Biting his neck. The blood surging into her mouth. Hot metal spilling into her throat. The taste of it. So nice. Making her feel a way she'd never felt before.

Making her want *more*.

That's it you can't resist you've seen it's better so you have to join us you have to join us and let us take you and you can be the same because we worship you we...

That voice again. Only it *sounded* like it was changing a bit now. Changing inside her. She didn't know what anger sounded like. But she felt like this might be what anger sounded like.

Like that voice was pleading with her.

Like it was begging her. Begging her to see sense.

And because it was begging her like that, it made her wonder whether she could trust it at all—

Yes trust it trust it trust it trust us trust...

And suddenly, she was in the darkness again. She was in the darkness, and she couldn't see anything. She couldn't *hear* anything, either. She was just in that dark hole, hovering, floating, and oh God, she felt like she'd been here before. She'd been here before, only the memory was furry, cloudy, and she couldn't remember why she'd been here or when she'd been here or where *here* even was, only that she had, and...

Suddenly, a figure.

Right in front of her.

A girl.

A girl. In a chair. Tied up. Chained at her wrists. Her eyes looked weird. Sort of like the marbles she sometimes stole from Dad and played with. She liked the feel of them when they banged into each other. They felt nice. Dad used to say they sounded nice, too. So she imagined what that might be like just based on the little shaking feeling in her fingers when they tapped against each other.

You're not alone.

A voice. In her head. Speaking to her. Not the same voice as before. A different one now. She could tell it was different because... well, she just could.

And this one sounded... *softer*. It sounded *nicer*.

It sounded...

You need to find me. We can stop this. Together.

The girl. The girl in the chair. In the chains. With the blood on her face. And the marble eyes. What did her words mean?

These sounds, coming from her mouth into Nisha's head, she didn't understand them. They were just noises.

But somehow... she understood them.

They turned to words in her head.

How can I find you? Nisha thought. Imagining the words. Imagining them right there in her head. And hoping the girl could see her too.

But then the girl started fading away. And even though noises were coming from her mouth, entering Nisha's head, she couldn't understand them anymore.

No. Please. Help.

The darkness started closing in.

The girl started fading away.

The darkness grew darker, the sounds suddenly disappeared, and Nisha was in the silence again.

Please. Please help. Please...

She tried to hold on to the image of that girl right in front of her.

She tried to make the jumble of sounds make sense.

She tried to keep the darkness light. Because she didn't want to disappear into the darkness. Not again. She wanted to stay here, and she wanted to stay awake, and...

The strength drifted out of her body.

An explosion of pain filled her chest.

And then, everything went black again.

KEIRA

* * *

Keira stumbled down the bridlepath with Nisha in her arms again, with Rufus by her side, and she wasn't sure how much longer she would be able to stay on her feet without collapsing from exhaustion.

It was late. Pitch black. The bridleway was overgrown, with tall, menacing trees on either side and a narrow, muddy pathway right down the middle. The rain was hammering down. She kept on seeing movement. Movement darting in the corners of her eyes. She swore she heard things, too. Groans. Gasps. Choking noises. And sometimes, voices. Voices that she was sure belonged to bad people. Cackling people. Evil people.

And now and then, she *smelled* it, too. That stench. That earthy stench, but not as pungent as normal. More just a whiff of it. A whiff of it from afar. And smelling it reminded her of the group. That huge group of infected she'd seen staggering through the field, right around that horrible, tainted moment she was trying not to think about.

Staggering towards them.

Then, running towards them.
Towards her, Dad, and Rufus.
And then...
Stopping.
Turning around.
And walking away.

She hadn't seen any infected since then. Had they all banded together in that larger group? It seemed unusual. It seemed like something from the realms of horror or science fiction.

But... fuck, Keira didn't understand anything about this virus. This virus—if it even *was* a virus—moved in different ways to other viruses. It was almost its own thing. It had its own rules. Its own reference points.

She remembered the mystery surrounding COVID when it first arrived on the scene. The fear of the unknown.

Well, take that and times it by unprecedented amounts, and you've pretty much landed on the mystery of this virus.

No warning.
No rules.
Just pure fear.

She'd seen some weird shit. Just earlier today, with Dad, she'd heard barking in a house, gone inside, and found it was an *infected* person making that sound.

And crying, too. But not like the infected cried. Crying like a human. Like a victim. Like it was imitating the last person it'd heard.

Before it killed them.

It made her shiver. She was trying not to think about that moment too much. She was trying not to think about a lot of moments right now.

She couldn't.

Because she had to keep her shit together. Nisha depended on it.

But there were only so many memories she could push down.

There were only so many things she could suppress. That she could hide away from.

Before they all came bursting up through the surface.

"Keira," Sarah said.

Keira heard the voice, and her stomach sank. She didn't want to be awful. She knew Sarah was realistic and pragmatic and all those things. And she knew Sarah cared about finding shelter, too. She cared about Nisha in her own subdued, borderline-autistic way.

But Keira heard the way she said her name. She heard the tone of her voice. And she couldn't be arsed dealing with whatever she had to say right now.

She had to keep going, Nisha in her arms, after Sarah carried her for a brief while. Sarah wanted to help out – bless her. But she was struggling with some pain of her own. Mystery pain.

And besides. Keira had to admit she was pretty pleased to be holding on to Nisha again.

She had to get her to safety.

She had to—

"Keira," Sarah said, grabbing her arm.

Keira stopped. Turned around. Holding on to Nisha as the rain lashed down from above. Sarah stared at her, wide-eyed. Pale.

"We've been walking all night. We need to rest."

"We'll rest when we find somewhere safe."

"We aren't going to find anywhere safe down a bridlepath in the middle of nowhere."

Keira felt Sarah's words like a punch to the gut. She was sick of Sarah being the voice of reason. She was right. She knew she was right. And being down here, out of the way, in the middle of nowhere, felt counteractive to what they were trying to achieve. They were trying to keep Nisha safe. They were trying to look after her. They needed rest. They *all* needed rest.

But at the same time... straying back into the suburbs or anywhere more populated was a recipe for disaster. She'd seen the kind of people there. If it wasn't the infected causing chaos, it was the looters and the gangs who pretty much ran the streets right now. It hadn't taken long for society to spiral out of control.

They couldn't take their chances. Not anymore.

They needed to find somewhere safe around here.

They needed to shelter around here.

Somewhere secluded.

Somewhere safe.

And then there was that helicopter.

She'd seen it in the distance when she stood beside Dad's dying body. Seen it landing. And as much as Sarah insisted they'd walked right past where it landed, it couldn't possibly have flown off again, or they would've noticed it. They'd have heard it. They'd have seen it. She didn't know where the fuck it'd gone. But she couldn't shake the feeling that they hadn't been looking quite closely enough.

Keira's arms were so heavy. Nisha wasn't heavy at all, but carrying someone for this length of time was enough to make it feel like she was carrying a ton of lead. But that wasn't stopping her. Nothing was stopping her.

"We find shelter," Sarah said. "In whatever form it comes in. Even if it's a sheltered bush or something. We need to rest, Keira. You need to rest."

Keira shook her head. Took another shaky step. "I've no time to rest."

"It's not just about you."

"What?"

"You're not the only person here. There's me. And there's Rufus, too. The dog. He needs rest, too. If we keep walking like this, we're going to exhaust ourselves. We're going to starve, and we're going to dehydrate. And what then? What happens to Nisha when we can't physically help her?"

Again, Keira felt this prick of heat in her face. This flicker of annoyance. She didn't want to agree with Sarah. She didn't want to see where she was coming from.

But she couldn't help *but* get what she was saying.

She was right. Sarah was right.

And that was the annoying thing.

That was the annoying fucking thing.

She looked down at Nisha, and she stopped. Nisha looked even paler, her skin glowing in the moonlight. The blood around her nostrils and her lips had crusted. She didn't look any better. She didn't look any closer to waking up and coming around. She was still breathing very lightly, which was pretty much Keira's only saving grace right now.

But she couldn't shake the feeling that something bad was going to happen. That the next time she checked Nisha, she wouldn't find a pulse. Or she wouldn't feel her breathing. And the realisation of what she'd lost would sneak up on her all over again. No, it wouldn't sneak up on her. It'd hit her like a ton of motherfucking bricks.

"I just don't want to waste any time," Keira said.

But she realised the futility of her words. Because how was she wasting time at all? She wasn't heading anywhere in particular. She was wandering aimlessly. They were all wandering aimlessly. All walking with this thin sense of, what, hope? Hope that they might just run into someone who could help Nisha?

And if they *did* help her, what then? What next? Nisha woke up. The cycle of surviving, fleeing from the infected, finding somewhere safe, facing destruction, and surviving all over again just repeated itself again and again and again. That was life now.

Was that a life she even wanted to live?

Was it a life *anyone* would want to live?

Maybe it was the grief. Maybe it was the shock. Maybe it was the exhaustion.

But right now, all the hope Keira clung so firmly onto felt like it was slipping between her fingers.

She stood there with Nisha in her arms as the rain fell heavily from above.

She looked into Sarah's eyes. Took a deep breath. And she went to speak.

That's when she saw it.

Right over Sarah's shoulder.

Movement.

A movement that she thought was just in her head at first. All in her imagination. She'd seen things already. Visions, amid her exhaustion.

And that's all this was.

Just another vision.

She was tired, and she was hungry, and she was dehydrated, and she'd been through so much shit, and she was seeing things.

But when she squinted further down the bridlepath, blinked, and cleared her eyes, she still saw that movement.

Moving towards them.

Walking at first.

And then, running.

"Sarah..." Keira started.

And that's when it hit her.

That's when Keira noticed it.

Not in her imagination anymore.

Not just a whiff.

But that *smell*.

That earthy smell.

It was strong.

It was getting stronger.

And it was racing closer towards them.

The infected.

The infected were here.

They were chasing them.

Again.

And they weren't giving up.

SARAH

* * *

When Sarah heard the groans and the growls creeping up the bridlepath, her stomach sank.

But there was an air of inevitability to those groans.

There was an air of inevitability to the dirty smell, inching closer towards her, towards Keira, and towards Rufus.

They'd evaded the infected for far too long. Probably the longest spell they'd gone without running into them since the outbreak began.

But they were here now. And it was hard to tell how many of them there were. She could see movement in the distance, in the dark. She could hear the groans. She could smell the dirtiness in her nostrils. And she could taste blood across her lips. Blood from where she'd been biting the sides of her mouth. Chewing the sides of her mouth, which she always did when stressed.

Dean used to know she was stressed by that marker. Honestly, she didn't even know she did it herself before he pointed it out. She remembered the nights she spent sitting on the sofa, waiting for him to come home from work, wondering what sort of mood he was going to be in. And even if he *were* in one sort of mood when he got home, he might not be in that same mood a few minutes or an hour later.

And it was always Sarah's fault. It was always her fault for not picking up on his mood, saying the wrong thing, or upsetting him.

And she couldn't really argue with him, could she? People had been telling her she got things wrong her entire life. So she didn't even question that he might be "gaslighting." Honestly, she didn't even know what that phrase meant until later in her life. She just automatically assumed he must be right and that she was the problem. Because she always *was* the problem. So why should things be any different with Dean?

He'd kiss her. And then he'd pull away. Frown in that look that could quite realistically go either way. "You've been biting again," he'd say, licking his lips. "You had a stressful day?"

And she didn't want to tell him that every day was stressful. That every day for her was a challenge. A challenge of trying to be normal for everyone else. And then trying to be normal for *him*. A challenge of trying her best to do the right thing, say the right thing, and look the right way... for *him*.

It took her so many years to realise that she could never do, be, or say the right thing.

Because there was no such thing as the right thing where Dean was concerned.

She could never, ever get things right where Dean was concerned.

Because he didn't *want* her to get things right.

She saw the figures drifting towards them up ahead. Her body ached. Like mad. Her feet. Her legs. Her chest. Her arms. Every inch of her. She wasn't sure she'd hurt this much since the day of the fall itself. The doctors always warned her not to push herself. That there were some "precarious skeletal situations" inside her—

his words—and that pushing herself could cause serious damage in both the short term and the long run.

She wasn't sure she was capable of running much further.

She wasn't sure how much further she could go.

But she looked around at Rufus, growling in that supposedly intimidating way, and at Keira, holding Nisha, and she felt this sense of duty. That was the only way she could really describe it. A sense of duty. Like this was the only thing she could do.

Like this was the *right* thing to do.

"You should go," Sarah said.

Keira frowned. "What?"

"I don't think I can make another step," Sarah said. "My body. It's... it's so sore. It's broken. I'm not going to make it. And you shouldn't stick around with me. You should run. All of you should run."

"Sarah—"

"If we all try to run together, we won't make it," Sarah said. Trying to be as rational as possible. "I'll hold you back."

Keira shook her head. "I'm not leaving you behind, too."

"Don't be stupid. You know better than anyone what Nisha is worth. You have to do what you have to do. For her. You know that. You knew that before anyone."

Keira shook her head. Tears oozed from her eyes again. Up the bridlepath, Sarah heard more of those infected, inching closer. The smell getting stronger. Time. Running out.

"You need to go," Sarah said. "And you can't look back."

Keira shook her head.

"Don't do something stupid for my benefit," Sarah said. "I'm making this decision. Me. So listen to me. Go. Now. And don't look back."

But Keira wasn't moving.

She was just standing there.

Shaking her head.

"Go!" Sarah shouted.

Keira looked down at Nisha, lying stationary in her arms.

She looked up at Sarah.

Then she looked over her shoulder.

Off into the distance.

Off into the darkness.

Towards those approaching infected.

And then, she took a deep breath and looked right at Sarah again.

"I can't," Keira said. "Take Nisha. Because I... I just can't."

Sarah felt her eyes widen. No. No, she couldn't do this. She had to run. She had to go. She had to take Nisha with her. Rufus... she was pretty sure he'd take himself away as the infected got closer.

But Keira couldn't do this.

"Keira," Sarah said. "Please. Go. Now. Don't do this."

Keira held Nisha close.

She took a long, deep breath, very audible.

And then she closed her eyes.

"I'm tired of people dying because of me," she said.

She looked at Keira.

She looked at Nisha.

She looked at Rufus.

And as her body ached, as her bones cracked and split with pain, and as her heart raced, Sarah tasted that blood in her mouth.

That blood, as she bit away at her cheeks.

The infected inched closer.

The growls grew louder.

The footsteps staggered within metres.

And all she could do was stand there and wait.

Wait for the pain.

Wait for the darkness.

Wait for the...

KEIRA

* * *

Keira held Nisha in her arms, watched the infected inch closer, and she smiled.

Tears streamed down her face. She felt broken. She felt exhausted. She felt weak. She felt like this was a nightmare, and it wasn't really happening to her. It was a bad dream. It was a bad dream, and soon she was going to wake up, and everything was going to be okay again. She'd be a child again. She'd be a child, and Mum and Dad would still be together, and she'd be able to live her entire life differently. So differently.

But for now, she was exhausted.

The infected raced down the dark bridleway towards her. Glowing in that moonlight. Lighting up under the glow of the stars. She didn't feel the same fear she might usually feel in a moment like this. There was just... an inevitability about it. She'd survived so long. She'd survived so long, and she'd protected Nisha as well as she could. But now her time was up. Everyone's time ran out, eventually. And this was her moment. This was where it ended. For her.

She wasn't special.

She wasn't different.

She'd made it this far. Partly through luck. Partly through circumstance.

But her time was about to run out.

And she felt okay about it.

She felt entirely okay about it.

Because she was drifting, she was dreaming, this wasn't real, this was...

There was something inside her.

And it was telling her not to move.

It was telling her to stand right here.

That standing right here was good for her.

That standing right here was good for everyone.

She closed her burning eyes. She didn't want to look at Sarah. She didn't want to see the fear on her face. She didn't want to see that urgency to her gaze. She wanted Keira to run. She wanted her to run with Nisha.

And she *wanted* to. Deep down, Keira knew it was right.

But run where?

Where would she go?

How much further could she keep on going?

She couldn't.

She couldn't go any further.

So all she could do was stand here with Nisha in her arms.

All she could do was hold her. For as long as she could hold her.

Protect her. For as long as she could protect her.

And all she could do was stand here with the knowledge that she'd tried her best. She'd tried her very best.

She'd fought.

She'd run.

She'd protected Nisha. And she'd gone so far to protect her. To so many lengths.

For Omar.
For Jean.
For Dad.
And for herself.
But now, her time was up.

The last few years flashed through her mind. Alone. Alone, moving from shitty flat to shitty flat. Days without eating. Drinking far too much. She thought of the nights she got too drunk. The nights she lay in the bath and wondered how long she could lie there without being noticed if she dunked her head under the water and drowned herself. Probably a long time. If it wasn't for work wanting her to be in, probably months.

She'd cut herself off from society, from work. She'd let friendships drift. She'd spent nights downloading, deleting, and re-downloading Tinder, seeking connection, seeking validation, growing terrified whenever she got too close to anyone, and blocking them without explanation. Her phone was littered with a list of numbers of men she'd ghosted. A cemetery of embarrassment. A grave of unexplored connection. A body of lost possibilities.

Ironically, the last few weeks—rebuilding that connection with Dad, growing closer to Nisha, and even getting to know Sarah a little—she'd felt more connected to the world than she'd felt in a long time.

She held Nisha close. The infected ran down the bridleway. She squeezed her eyes shut. Felt Nisha's cold, wet body pressed right up against hers.

And she couldn't think right now. She couldn't rationalise any of her actions.

All she saw were the last few weeks flashing before her eyes.

All she saw was all the pain she'd been through, all the loss she'd witnessed.

All she saw was all the suffering she'd been surrounded by.

And all the suffering that would chase her through this world, no matter how far she ran.

But she was exhausted.

She was tired.

She was done.

"It's okay, Nisha," she muttered. "It's okay. Everything will be okay soon. Everything will be okay. Everything will be…"

NISHA

* * *

Nisha didn't *hear* anything this time.

But she saw something again.

From the darkness, she saw something. The moon. The moon shining down bright from above. And she was on some sort of path somewhere. Some sort of path in the middle of nowhere. She didn't know where she was. She felt cold. She wanted to sleep. She wanted nothing more than to sleep for a long, long time in a nice comfy bed.

But she was walking again.

And she was walking *inside* someone again.

Seeing through someone else's eyes.

She looked down at her body. It was moving without her control. It was a lady this time. A lady maybe as old as her mum would've been. Maybe it was Mum. She hadn't seen Mum in years. She didn't know where she'd gone. Didn't know where she'd moved to. Dad didn't tell her much about Mum. He just told her that it had nothing to do with Nisha, which always made Nisha think it must be something to do with her because he kept saying it too much, and sometimes when people said things too much, even if it was the opposite to what they were saying, they were trying to say the... God, even she'd lost herself now, but she knew what she meant.

She looked down at her body, and she wondered if this was a dream. It didn't feel like a dream. It felt real. So real. She'd done this a few times now. Entered the brains of the bad people. That's what it felt like she was doing. She'd done it back when Sarah was in trouble with the army man. And then she'd done it with *all* those bad people running towards David, Keira, and Rufus. Somehow, she'd got into *all* their heads, and then she'd turned them away even though they wanted to get to her friends, and...

Yes. That's when it was. That's the last thing she remembered in real life, not in this weird dream bad person world. She'd seen some weird things. She'd been in the heads of more bad people. She'd seen things through the eyes of the bad people. And maybe that's what was special about her. She was special because she'd been bitten and hadn't turned into a bad person, and she was special because even before she was bitten, she could stop the bad people attacking her and other people without even thinking about it.

But this. This was something else. This was different.

And then there was the girl.

The thought of the girl made her feel shivery.

The girl.

Speaking to her.

Sitting there in that dark room, chained up.

Looking at her with her marble eyes.

Saying *words* to her. Words she could *hear*. And words that, for some reason, right away, she could understand. She hadn't heard noises before; she hadn't heard sounds before. But for some reason, it was like this girl was speaking words into her head. Writing them in her head so she could understand them.

You need to find me. We can stop this. Together.

There was something about that girl.

For some reason, she wanted to get to her.

She wanted to reach her.

She didn't know where she was. But she needed to.

Because there was the other voice, too.

The other voice that made her feel nervous.

The voice that felt like her own thoughts. Her own mind.

The voice that was more like... pictures in her head.

Pictures. Telling her what to do.

And right now, even though she couldn't *HEAR* the words, she could feel the thoughts growing as she walked down this path.

She could *feel* herself getting closer to... well, *herself*.

And she could *feel* what that voice wanted her to do.

It wanted her to bite herself.

It wanted her to bite herself, and then it wanted her to bite her somewhere that would do real damage and...

She didn't know. She didn't know after that. Just that deep in her belly, she knew that biting herself somewhere that'd do her real damage was bad news.

She stumbled further down the path, in this woman's body, when she noticed something.

Sarah.

Standing there.

Looking right at her in this bad person's body.

Then Keira.

Holding *her* in her arms.

Herself.

Her own body.

Nisha's body.

And then she saw Rufus.

Barking. Opening his mouth wide and barking, even though she couldn't hear him.

She watched them all get closer, and she realised she wasn't staggering. She was running.

Running fast.

Running fast towards them.

She tensed up her body. And it felt like she was tensing up her *own* body; even though she wasn't inside her body, she was inside someone else's body, one of the bad people's bodies.

No don't fight it let it happen they're willing and ready let it happen my dear let it happen and everything will be joyous...

The feeling. More a feeling than a voice. Deep in her chest.

The feeling that was so strong.

The feeling that made her run faster.

Run towards Sarah.

Run towards Keira.

Run towards—

Herself.

She wanted to bite herself she wanted to rip her throat out she wanted to *TASTE*.

Taste the blood and fly with the bats and bite them and rip them all open and bathe in them and—

No.

No!

She didn't want that.

She didn't want that 'cause she was Nisha.

She was Nisha, and she was a good person.

She wasn't a bad person.

But the longer she spent in the bad people's heads, the more she felt like she was a bad person after all.

The longer she spent in their heads, the stronger that feeling grew.

She needed to wake up.

She needed to stop the bad people, and then she needed to wake up, and she needed to tell the others about what she'd seen and about the girl.

But for now, she ran.

She ran towards Sarah. And even though usually she felt like she could stop the bad people running, stop herself running, she couldn't now. It was like she was watching a video game that someone else was playing. That Dad was playing.

Only it was a video game where Dad was playing as the bad guy, and he was about to do something really bad.

She tried to close her eyes, but she couldn't.

She tried to hold her breath, but she couldn't.

She tried to stop herself, but she just couldn't.

Don't fight it don't resist it let it happen let it happen and—

The girl.

A flash of the girl in her head.

A glimpse of her marble eyes.

And the *SOUND* of her voice.

A voice that she understood.

"I'm with you," she said. "I'm..."

And then Nisha felt a sharp pain in the middle of her body, as she opened her mouth, as she threw herself towards Sarah, as she went to bury her teeth into her throat...

SARAH

* * *

Sarah held the blade as the infected woman raced towards her.

She wasn't going out without a fight.

Even though there were a ton of these fuckers launching themselves towards her, towards Keira, towards Nisha, and towards Rufus, she wasn't admitting defeat.

She wasn't standing here and accepting defeat.

Even though she was in pain. Even though her entire body ached—no, *worse* than ached...

She was fighting.

She was going down fighting.

The infected ran towards her.

Blood oozing from their lips.

Chunks of pale flesh dangling from their limbs.

A chorus of skin-crawling shrieks.

But then something happened.

The woman.

She stopped.

Right in front of her.

She stopped, and she just stood there. Frozen. Staring not exactly *at* Sarah. But rather *through* her.

The smell of the earthy dirtiness built even stronger. The taste of sweat stung her lips and made her feel sick. The agony crippled her body. Her shoulders. Her back. Her legs. Every inch of her splitting with pain.

But she held that knife.

She held it, and she braced herself.

Braced herself to swing it at the infected woman and...

She just froze.

She stood there. Staring off into the distance. Sarah's heart raced. What was this? Was this the calm before the storm? Only... no, this woman wasn't the only one frozen still. The others. The ones right behind her. They were all frozen, too. Standing there. Not budging. Not moving a single muscle.

And it didn't make sense. She couldn't understand it. The only time she'd seen this was when...

Wait.

Nisha.

She turned around.

Looked into Keira's arms.

And she saw her.

Nisha.

Eyes open.

Wide open.

Her pupils rolled back into her skull.

Fresh blood oozing out of the corners of her eyes.

Rolling down the sides of her face.

She was doing this.

Somehow, she was doing it again.

She was stopping them.

Even though she was unconscious, she was holding them back.

How was she doing it? Sarah didn't have a clue. And honestly, she didn't really care.

She was doing it. That was the main thing. That really was the only thing that mattered here.

And they had to make it count.

She looked back around at the infected. Saw them shaking a little. Saw their mouths moving. It looked like they might be breaking free of their stupor. Shit. They needed to get away. They needed to get away while they still had a chance.

She looked back at Keira. Who looked down at Nisha. Wide-eyed. Like she was realising what was happening here, too.

"Quick," Sarah gasped. "We need to run. We need to get away from here. We need to go. Now!"

She grabbed Keira's arm, and she turned her around, and they ran together down this bridleway. Rufus beside them. Together.

She didn't want to look over her shoulder. Didn't want to look back. She didn't want to face the infected again. They'd been lucky. They should be dead right now. Or... worse. They should be being attacked right now. Teeth sinking into their skin as they lay helplessly on the muddy ground, screaming in agony. The thought of the pain she should be suffering right now. The pain she should be going through right now if Nisha hadn't somehow helped her again out of nowhere.

Shit. She couldn't let the anxiety cripple her. Even though that was easier said than done. The thought of it filled her with dread. Sheer dread.

They were lucky. So fortunate.

But now they needed to make that fortune count.

They needed to get away.

And they needed to get away fast.

Suddenly, she heard something. A gasp. A groan. Right behind her. She didn't want to look over her shoulder. But she couldn't help herself.

She looked back. Saw a couple of infected towards the back

running now. Hard to make out properly in the darkness. But she didn't have to. Sprinting. Getting closer towards them and not stopping for anything.

"Shit," Sarah said. "They're coming. Come on."

Keira was running. Running alongside her down this darkened bridleway. But she was looking down at Nisha, too. Looking at those wide-open eyes. Looking at those burst blood vessels creeping through the whites of her eyes. Looking at the blood oozing down her temples and into her hair.

"She'll be okay," Sarah gasped. Even though she had absolutely no justification for that statement other than pure sentiment.

They just needed to take this opportunity.

They just needed to get away.

And they needed to be quick about it.

She ran around a corner. Raced down towards the road. It was a country lane. But a road was still a dangerous place. There could be infected down there. There were houses down there, so the chances of running into someone or something were a possibility.

But they didn't have a choice right now.

They couldn't be selective right now.

They had to get down this pathway.

They had to get to the road.

They had to—

Suddenly, Sarah saw something right up ahead.

Movement.

More movement.

Her heart raced. Her chest tightened. She didn't want to stop running. But she froze.

Because right up ahead, right up the road, she saw more movement.

She found herself praying. As her stomach turned, as her heart raced faster, and as the intensity of the anxiety grew inside her, she found herself praying to herself.

Please don't be infected. Please, please don't be infected.

She stared up the path.

Stared towards those figures. Blocking their only way out as the rest of the infected broke free of their Nisha-induced stupor and got closer.

Please don't...

And then she saw something that filled her with even more dread.

The figures ahead.

They all twitched.

They all screamed.

And then, just like that, they all ran.

They were infected.

And they were coming for Sarah.

For Keira.

For Nisha.

For Rufus.

And this time, this time... there really was no way out.

They were trapped.

And there was no escape.

KEIRA

* * *

One moment, Keira felt like she was sleeping.

Like she was dreaming.

Like she was indoctrinated, engulfed, swallowed up by shock and grief, and in no control of her actions. In no control of *anything*.

And the next, suddenly, out of nowhere, she was awake again.

She was alive again.

Free of the haze.

The infected. Frozen. Frozen still. She'd seen them freeze like that before. And the times they'd frozen like that?

The only times she'd seen that happen... Nisha was involved.

She looked down at Nisha, and suddenly, she saw what was happening.

Nisha's eyes weren't closed. For the first time since she'd been reunited with her—since Sarah came wandering across the field with her in her arms, holding her—her eyes were open.

But that didn't mean she was awake.

Her eyes were rolled back into her skull. The whites of her

eyes were red. Burst blood vessels. And blood oozed out of her eyelids, a little out of her nostrils, too.

But it was *something*.

It was something *more* than a few seconds prior.

She was, in a way, awake.

And somehow, even though she was unconscious, she was still managing to hold the infected back.

"Quick!" Sarah shouted. And Keira didn't understand. Not at first.

Not until she looked around and saw Sarah running towards her.

Because the infected were breaking free of their stupor.

"Now!" Sarah shouted.

Keira turned around, and she ran. Held on to Nisha and ran. Ran with Sarah, who grabbed her arm. Ran with Rufus right beside her. Ran down the muddy bridlepath as the rain continued to hammer down.

She'd almost stood there, and she'd almost let the infected take her. Sarah. Sarah wanted to protect her. She wanted to sacrifice herself for her. For Nisha. For Rufus. But Keira couldn't let that happen. She couldn't just leave her to die. She couldn't just leave her on her own. She couldn't let someone else die for her. She couldn't leave anyone else behind. Not again.

But now she was awake again. She was awake. She couldn't make sense of the stupor she'd fallen into. Was it the shock? Was it the exhaustion? Or was it... something else?

The infected. There was so much Keira didn't know about them. There was so little *everyone* knew about them.

Maybe they were capable of far, far more than she first feared.

Than *everyone* first feared.

And now she was running. Running down the bridleway. Running away from the oncoming infected. Who snarled. And shrieked. Getting closer and closer and...

Keira, Sarah, and Rufus turned the corner. And they ran

further down the pathway. She didn't know where this led. But it didn't really matter. All that mattered right now was getting away.

She looked down at Nisha. Her eyes were closing a little. Her pupils shifting back into place.

"Stay with me," Keira said. "You just hold on in there. It's going to be okay. Everything's going to be okay."

She looked up and noticed something.

Sarah. She wasn't running anymore. She was still. Completely still. Which... Fuck. She couldn't freeze. Not now. The infected were breaking free of their haze. They were rounding the corner. They were going to get them. They were going to surround them. They had a second chance. They had a second chance, and they had to take it. They had to get away.

But then she saw something down the path, and she understood.

More infected.

Running down the path.

Towards them.

"We're trapped," Sarah said. She looked at Keira with a pale face and wide eyes. She looked at Nisha, then back at the infected rounding the corner. She looked at Rufus, who barked and then whined a little, his bravado making way for fear.

"We can't be trapped," Keira said. Looking to her right. At the hedge. But it was solid. It was thick. There was no getting through those branches. There was no way through at all.

The infected ran closer.

From up ahead.

And from behind.

"I don't see a way out," Sarah said.

But... No.

Keira was back out of that shock state now—or whatever the hell that state was.

She was awake.

And she wasn't giving up.

"I can't just give up."

She tried to drag the branches of the hedge aside.

She looked over her shoulder.

Then ahead.

She watched these rage-fuelled figures race closer towards them all.

She looked to the left.

She looked to the right.

But the infected were closing in.

Time was running out.

She stood there, shaking, shivering, as the earthiness surrounded her.

She held Nisha in her arms.

She didn't want to apologise to her.

She didn't want to lose her.

But she didn't know what the hell to do right now.

She stood there as the infected approached, as time ran out, as options diminished, and...

Suddenly, up the path, she heard something unexpected.

A bang.

No. Not just a bang.

But a series of bangs.

And it sounded louder than pretty much anything she'd ever heard. Kind of like fireworks going off. Only...

No. These weren't fireworks.

She knew what they were. But they weren't fireworks.

These were bullets.

Gunfire.

She looked around.

The infected chasing them were falling. Those who hadn't yet fallen were turning around. Turning their attention to... Fuck. Torchlights.

They were turning their attention to the people shooting at them in the darkness.

"Torchlights," Sarah muttered.

But Keira didn't hear her. She could only watch as the infected fell. And then, as the infected behind them both got even closer, she could only run.

Run towards that gunfire with Nisha in her arms.

Run towards them as they gunned down the infected up ahead.

"We're not infected!" Keira shouted. Desperate. Clinging to the briefest of hope.

Racing towards the lights.

Racing towards those fallen infected.

Racing towards the figures in the distance.

The figures turned their lights right at Keira, Sarah, Nisha, and Rufus.

The infected chased behind them. And she knew how this would look. A crowd of infected. A crowd of infected that they were right at the front of. They were going to get lost in the crowd. They were going to get gunned down. They were going to get gunned down, and even if these people didn't gun them down, they were drawing these infected right to their position.

"We're not infected!" Keira shouted. The loudest damned shout she'd ever screamed. "We're not infected. Please!"

They ran towards the lights as these figures raised their rifles.

They ran closer towards them as they steadied their aim.

"We're not..."

And then, the people ahead steadied their aim, pulled their triggers, and opened fire.

SARAH

* * *

It all happened so fast.
Sarah watched the infected race down the bridlepath, race towards her. Race towards Keira. Race towards Nisha. Race towards Rufus.

She heard the infected snarling and shouting and crying out behind her as they ran closer, as they closed in. Surrounded them. Surrounded them on both sides.

A knot tightened in her stomach. Her heart raced. The taste of vomit filled her mouth, burning stomach acid stinging the back of her lips.

This was happening.

This was happening, and there was nothing she was going to be able to do about it.

There was nothing *any* of them could do about it.

She held her breath and stood by Keira's side and...

And then it happened.

The lights.

The lights appearing out of nowhere.

And then the explosions. Like fireworks. Like... gunfire.

And then the infected racing down the bridlepath, racing towards them, they started to fall. They started to collapse. Like a deck of cards. Falling. Falling, one after another.

Someone was helping them.

Someone was *shooting* the infected.

She heard that gunfire rattling on. And tension began to grow in her chest. Because they had to run down this pathway. But running down this pathway was going to be dangerous. It was going to be a risk. A real risk. Because those bullets. They were running into the line of fire. They were running into the line of fire, and they were risking everything.

But what other choice did they have?

"We need to be careful," Sarah shouted. But right as she shouted those words, Keira started running. Nisha in her arms. Rufus by her side.

"We're not infected!" Keira shouted, racing towards them.

Sarah gulped. It was a risk. But they didn't have a choice. Time was running out. They needed to get the hell down this bridlepath. They needed to get the hell away from the infected.

But those people.

Those people with the torches.

Those people with the guns.

She thought of the men on the road.

The military men.

The men who'd held those rifles to her head.

Who'd threatened Nisha.

What if they were the same people?

But... Hell. As unappealing as being caught up with those men might be right now, it was infinitely preferable to the thought of being torn to shreds by the infected masses.

She swallowed another thick, heavy lump in her throat.

And then she started running again, after Keira, after Rufus, and towards that gunfire, towards the falling infected, towards—

She felt a hand tighten around her arm. Yanking her back. Sending her off balance.

She tried to stay on her feet. She tried to hold her ground.

But there was nothing she could do.

She tumbled over. Slammed against the ground, splattered in the mud. She swung around onto her back.

An infected woman.

Pinning her down.

Blood oozing down her cheeks from her eyes.

Her mouth wide.

Her teeth yellow and covered in blood.

Screaming.

Screaming right in Sarah's face.

She opened her mouth, and she moved towards Sarah's throat as more of the infected rushed down the path towards her. She tried to pin the infected man back, as her body ached, as her spine *wracked* with agony.

She tried to hold the infected woman back with her weak, shaking arms as its open mouth descended, closer and closer towards her neck.

"We're not infected!" Keira shouted, her voice drifting off into the distance. Rufus barking beside her. "We're not..."

And then more gunshots.

More gunshots, and more screams, and...

And then suddenly Sarah was back there again.

Back there on the ground again. After falling off that wall. Only she was in the memory she suppressed now. She was in the memory she didn't want to revisit.

She was on the ground.

And Harry Westwood was the only one left with her.

Sitting by her side as she lay there.

Football under his arm.

"It's okay," he said. This boy who teased her no end. This boy who bullied her into submission. He was here now. Here, by her side, as she lay there in pain.

Only he was moving his hands up her legs.

Moving his cold, long-fingernailed hands up the inside her of her bare thighs.

"It's okay," he said. "You're gonna be okay."

He moved his hands further up her legs, and she tried to move. She tried to shake free of him. She tried to get up. She tried to run. As she lay there. As her heart pounded.

But she couldn't.

She just couldn't move a muscle.

And that was the final torment.

That was the secret she'd never been able to tell anyone.

That moment was the secret she'd never been able to share, even with herself.

"It's okay," Harry's voice whispered in her ears as his hands crept further up her legs. "It'll all be okay..."

She closed her burning eyes.

She gritted her teeth.

She listened to the infected woman screaming right above her as her snapping jaw got closer and closer.

And then...

Gunshots.

A splatter of warmth right over her face. And then the pressure. The pressure from the arm of the infected. And the snarling. Gone. All gone.

She opened her eyes.

The infected woman. Her head. It wasn't... it wasn't even *there* anymore. It'd exploded. She was perched over Sarah, blood spurting out of her neck.

Something had happened to her.

Someone had *shot* her.

"Quick!" a voice shouted. Not Keira. Someone else. It sounded like... like a man.

And that made her distrustful. Instinctively, it made her sceptical. Because she didn't trust men. She didn't trust any men. Not after all the things she'd been through at the hands of men.

But right now, the prospect of men was far more appealing than the prospect of being torn to fucking shreds by the infected.

Just.

She pushed the infected woman's flimsy, bleeding body away.

She scrambled out from underneath her.

And then she saw them.

More of them.

More of those infected.

Running down the bridlepath.

Running closer towards her.

"Come on!"

That voice. Again.

She staggered up to her feet.

She looked at that oncoming mass of infected. Hurtling down the bridlepath now.

And then she ran.

She felt the splitting pain shooting up her shins.

She felt the tightness, the vice grip, the knives, and the blades stabbing their way up her thighs.

She felt the pain.

The pain right down her spine.

Harry's fingers on her thighs.

Dean's hands around her throat.

And that crippling sense of worthlessness, making every impossible step even harder.

"You can do this," she gasped as she ran down the bridlepath.

As she ran from the approaching infected.

As she ran from the cries.

As she ran towards the lights.

Towards the figures.

Away from the darkness.

"You can do this. You're okay. Everything is going to be okay…"

The infected got closer.

The snarls got louder.

And the voices in her head turned to screams.

"You can do this," she said as her legs failed her. As her back gave in. "You can…"

And then she tumbled towards the ground.

Fell face flat.

Right in the mud.

KEIRA

* * *

Keira watched Sarah stagger to her feet and run towards her.

The infected closing in behind her.

Rain lashed down heavily. There was no light anymore from the moon or the stars. Thick grey clouds suffocated any light. The only light? The light from the torches of these people—whoever they were—lighting up the infected, running towards them.

Lighting up Sarah as she limped along, staggered along, trying to stay on her feet.

Rain dripped down Sarah's hair. Her hair clung to her face. Not just water. But blood, too. Shit. These people. They'd fired at that infected woman hovering over her. Her head exploded all over Sarah. She'd seen people turn after contact with blood before, hadn't she? Back at the house, all the way back on the first day. The basement. The way the man whose name she couldn't even *remember* turned. The way he attacked everyone down there. *Everyone.*

Although… she hadn't seen anyone turn from contact with blood since. Not in her experience, anyway.

So she didn't know.

But Sarah.

On her feet.

Limping away from the infected.

Gasping.

Struggling to stay standing.

Clearly in pain.

Clearly in agony.

But still staggering along.

Keira stood there. Shaking. Frozen. The chorus of infected cries filled her ears. She could hear muffled talking. Talking between these people, whoever they were. Shit. She hadn't even had the chance to properly look at them as she stood there, Nisha in her arms. She hadn't even had the chance to assess who the hell they were.

All she saw were the lights.

All she heard were those guns.

That, for now, was enough.

And then it all happened so fast.

Sarah.

Losing her balance.

Tumbling to the ground.

Landing face flat in the mud.

The infected drifting closer and closer towards her.

Keira lunged forward. "Sarah!"

A hand. Grabbing her arm. Stopping her from moving another single step.

"We need to get away."

Keira looked at this man. She didn't have long to study him. He was muscular. He was balding. He looked about mid-thirties, maybe. And he had a scar right across his left cheek that told stories of conflict, stories of war.

And he was wearing a military uniform.

Holding a rifle.

She yanked her arm away from him. Pulled Nisha closer to her. Beside them both, Rufus barked. Growled. And whined a bit. Clearly eager to get away.

"I'm not leaving her," Keira said.

She turned around, holding Nisha.

The infected closing in on Sarah, who lay there, wincing in the mud.

Looking up at Keira. Pain in her eyes.

Fear in her eyes.

"There's too many of them," the man barked. "We need to get out of here. We need to get away. Please, lady. We're trying to help you. But we can't help you if you're dead."

She looked back around at him. He sounded genuine. He sounded legitimate. And the five, six other men with him... they all looked like him—dressed in the same way, anyway. All holding rifles. Clearly all military.

She held on to Nisha, and she saw herself at a crossroads.

She saw a decision opening up in front of her.

Nisha.

Getting her to safety.

What if these people *were* safety?

But at the same time...

She couldn't just hand Nisha over to some people she didn't even know. Regardless of how legit or benevolent they might seem.

But Sarah...

She looked down at Sarah.

Looked at her lying there.

Lying in the mud.

The infected getting closer.

"Go," she mouthed. "Before it's too late."

Keira shook her head. She felt Sarah's words like a dagger to the heart. Here she was. Someone else telling her to run. Telling her to leave her behind.

But Keira couldn't.

She couldn't leave her behind.

She couldn't leave anyone else behind.

She was done leaving people behind.

But...

Nisha.

Rufus.

"We need to go!" Another voice. Not the man who'd spoken to her. One of the other guys. And when Keira looked around, she saw some of these guys backing off. Running away.

But the man who'd spoken to her.

He was still standing there.

Still staring right at her.

Still holding his rifle.

"We need to go," he said. But he didn't sound demanding. He sounded more like he was begging. More like he was *pleading*.

She looked back at him.

She looked down at Nisha. Lying so peacefully in her arms. Lying so *still* in her arms.

And then she took a deep breath, turned around, looked right at Sarah, and...

Sarah stared up at Keira.

Her eyes twinkled in the torchlights.

"Go."

And then the infected all clambered right on top of her and engulfed her.

SARAH

* * *

It all happened so fast.

Sarah slammed against the damp, muddy ground. Mud splashed up over her face. She could taste it, strong and bitter on her lips. And she could smell it, too. The mixture of the mud, and the earthiness of the infected. All of it mixing together, all of it knocking her sick.

She stared up into the lights. She looked up and saw Keira standing there, holding on to Nisha. Looking down at her with those wide, terrified eyes. Shaking her head.

And behind her, Sarah heard the infected. Screaming. Their footsteps slapping against the muddy earth. So close to reaching her. So close to mounting on top of her, just like that infected woman earlier.

She looked at Nisha. Lying there, resting in Keira's arms.

And then she looked back up at Keira. Right into her eyes.

There was only one thing she could say.

There was only one thing she could do.

There was only one thing that mattered now.

And it was their safety.

"Go," Sarah said.

Keira shook her head. She tried to wrestle free of the man right beside her. The man with the light and the rifle. Pointing it right at her. But some of those other men, they were backing away. Running away.

"Go," Sarah repeated.

And then the smell of earthiness completely surrounded her, filled her nostrils, and the taste of it crept into her mouth, and the sound of their cries and screams spiralled around her, and...

Sarah didn't see what happened next.

Because she felt them.

The infected.

Landing on her.

One, by one, by one.

Knocking the wind out of her chest.

Crushing her.

Pressing her to the ground.

And she squeezed her eyes shut, and she waited for the splitting pain as the shouts echoed in the distance, and as Rufus's barks grew louder, and...

Bang.

Another bang.

Blood.

Blood.

Splattering all over her.

Hot blood splattering over her as the infected continued to descend on her.

As they continued to land on her.

A voice. Louder now. "We need to fall back!"

But Sarah could see what was happening.

Even though she was lying on the ground, going through it all... it was like she was watching events unfold on a television screen. Detached from her body, somehow.

The man. The one by Keira's side.

He was pointing his rifle towards the infected, who were landing on top of Sarah.

And he was pulling his trigger.

Pulling his trigger at every one of them.

Shooting at them.

He was helping her.

He lowered his rifle. But the echoes were still getting louder. The footsteps were still approaching. The infected were still coming. "You need to run!" he shouted. "Now!"

Her. He was speaking to her. He was telling her to get up. But how was she supposed to get up when she was in so much pain? Her legs burning with agonising intensity. Her back splitting with pain. Like knives were stretching their way right down the length of it, slipping between every single disc.

But she heard another series of blasts. Another series of bangs. And she felt more blood splattering over her. And saw more infected bodies tumbling to her side.

"Get up!" the man shouted. "Now!"

Sarah didn't have time to think anymore.

She didn't have time to be in any pain anymore.

She couldn't think about pain.

She could only focus on getting away.

She stood up. And even though the pain was so bad, even though the agony was so strong, she ran.

She staggered down the pathway.

Stumbled away from the last infected standing.

Gritting her teeth.

Biting the sides of her mouth.

It's just pain. It's just pain. It can't harm you... it's just sensation.

The man holding the rifle went to fire another bullet. And then he looked down at his gun, wide-eyed. "Fuck. Out of ammo. Fall back!"

He grabbed Keira's arm. She looked at Sarah as she held on to Nisha.

"It's okay," Keira said. "We're gonna be okay now."

And Sarah nodded. Even though the pain was splitting, even though the agony was so intense, she nodded.

She was going to be okay.

They were both going to be okay.

Everything was gonna be okay, and…

And then, suddenly, from the right, an infected man appeared.

Right between Sarah and Keira.

Right between her and her way out.

"Sarah!" Keira shouted.

The man with the rifle dragged Keira away as she held on to Nisha.

The infected man blocked Sarah's way.

Stood in her way.

Snarling.

Blood oozing from his torn lips.

Dripping from his eyes.

His once white shirt torn and stained red, and a nasty bite wound right on the middle of his shoulder.

"Sarah!" Keira echoed.

And as the infected man ran towards Sarah, there was nothing she could do but stand there.

Nothing she could do but watch.

Nothing she could do but wait as Keira, Nisha, and Rufus were dragged away into the darkness, into the rain.

She was alone.

KEIRA

* * *

Keira had no idea how long she'd been staggering in the torrential rain with these military men holding Nisha in her arms.

But she couldn't stop looking over her shoulder.

And not because of the infected. Not because of the infected at all. As much of a threat as they were, it wasn't the infected she was thinking of. It wasn't the infected she was worried about right now. Not so much. Not right now. Not in this haze of shock. This mist of loss.

It was Sarah.

She'd seen Sarah collapse in the middle of that bridleway however long ago it was now. Had to be an hour ago at least. Although maybe even longer. It felt like forever ago. She'd fallen. Hit the mud. And this man—this military man, with his rifle—he'd popped the heads of as many infected as he could. Tried to help her.

He'd begged Sarah to get up. Screamed at her to join him, to join his people.

And Keira shouted at her, too. Shouted at her to get up. To fight.

And Sarah got up. Of course, she got up. She got to her feet. She got to her feet, and she staggered towards Keira. Towards the military guys. Towards freedom—even if it was only a temporary freedom, it was still something.

And then...

The infected man.

Launching out of the bushes.

Running towards her.

And the small group of infected, still chasing her from behind.

She was surrounded.

She was surrounded, and there was no way out.

Keira saw the look on Sarah's face. She saw that fear in her eyes. She was such an emotionally guarded woman, sure. She had so many layers, layers that Keira hadn't even begun to see beneath, not yet.

But she could see she was afraid.

And at the same time, she could see something else, too.

That look.

That look in her eyes.

She might be scared. She might be afraid. But she wanted Keira to run. She wanted her to take Nisha. To protect her.

She looked down at Nisha. Lying there in her arms. Eyes closed again. Breathing—but barely.

Was she protecting her?

Had she done anything at all for her?

She looked up, then. Saw a building up ahead. Kind of looked like an old military bunker, rising out of the earth. Covered in grass over the top of it, with rusty, peeling old green doors and air vents on top of it. It looked disused. There were signs up all around it. Signs pointing to a vet next door. The bunker itself looked unguarded. Definitely not the sort of safe place Keira had in mind. More... makeshift than anything.

But it would do.

The man walked up to her—the man with the scar. The one who'd helped her. Tried to help Sarah. "We're here," he said.

And Keira nodded. It was all she could do. She was exhausted. She was still in shock. In shock from all the loss. First, Dad. Now, Sarah. And Nisha. Lying in her arms. Clinging to life.

She looked down at Nisha, then her eyes moved to her leg. To the bite on her leg. Covered at the moment. Good. That's what she needed. Now wasn't the time to tell the people here about Nisha's bite. She needed to assess these people first. She needed to figure out whether she could trust them. She couldn't go risking Nisha's life.

Honestly, more than anything, right now, she just needed rest.

She just needed to be alone.

She just needed shelter.

She just needed to process what she'd been through.

What she'd lost.

And Nisha needed help.

"The place we've got," the man said as they walked closer to these green gates. "It ain't much. But we're working on it. Okay? I can't promise we've got stacks of food. I can't promise we've got stacks of much at all. But there's good people there. And we're doing what we can to keep things under control. To keep people safe. You can trust us. Okay?"

Keira looked into his eyes. And even though she didn't know a thing about this man—she didn't even know his name, for Christ's sake—she felt a sincerity to his words. For the first time in weeks, an actual outsider whom she felt comfortable with immediately.

And the worst thing about that?

It just made her question him even more.

"Thank you," she said. Her lips shaking. Trying her best to keep her shit together and failing miserably. She was supposed to be tough. She was supposed to be strong. Not just for Nisha. But for herself.

And now she was acting like a victim.

She was acting weak.

She was acting... pathetic.

Because she didn't know who these people were. They'd saved her life, and they'd saved Nisha's life, and they'd saved Rufus's life. But beyond that, she didn't know a thing about them.

And maybe it was her desperation to find shelter. Maybe it was the sadness settling in after losing Dad. The shock wearing off, and the reality of her situation—the loneliness and the emptiness of her situation—all sneaking up on her. All clouding her judgement. All debilitating her actions.

But whatever it was... Keira found herself wanting to trust this man.

Wanting to trust these people.

Wanting to believe they could be good.

Because the alternative was crippling.

The alternative was exhausting.

"My name's Kevin," the man said. "We can talk about who we are and whatever once you get inside and get some rest. I just want you... I just want you to know you can be comfortable. If this ain't for you, you can walk away, okay? You can always walk away. But I really hope you don't. For your own sake." He looked down at Nisha. "And for the girl's sake."

Keira stood at the gates now. Rain poured down from above. This grass-covered bunker jutted out of the earth like some kind of relic from the Cold War era. People wandered around outside. Armed guards. Military. A few green military vehicles parked up. The smell of cigarette smoke and fruity vapes filled the air, intermingled with a strong aroma of sweat. It looked like this place was organised. Way more organised than anywhere she'd seen in recent weeks. And right now... right now, it felt like that would do.

"And I'm sorry," Kevin said. "About your friend. We tried... we tried what we could. I wish we could've kept trying. I'm sorry."

And Keira didn't even have the energy to be mad at him for

dragging her away from Sarah as the infected surrounded her. She wanted to. She really fucking wanted to.

But this guy had just been trying to help.

He'd helped her get away. He'd helped Nisha get away. He'd helped Rufus get away.

Sarah wasn't so lucky.

And Keira was going to have to try and live with that.

Another trauma to try and live with.

"I want to ask you again," Kevin said as they stood at the gates, the moon breaking through the clouds now. "You don't have to join us. But... I think it's in your best interests if you do. It's a dark world out here. I'm sure you've seen some shit. We have too. But it's better in here. We can help you. We're good people. There's order here. There's people like you. There's kids. Families. Supplies ain't exactly abundant. But we're doing our best. For everyone. Because if we lose our humanity... what hope do we have? What hope does anyone have?"

Keira looked into Kevin's eyes. Kind eyes. Friendly eyes. Soft eyes. Contrasting the scars on his face.

She looked over her shoulder into the dark. Into the rain. She swore she saw movement. She swore she heard distant groans. She swore she smelled the earthy stench. She swore she tasted death.

She gulped.

She turned around to Kevin.

She looked into his eyes.

"Okay," she said, nodding. Almost defeated.

Kevin's eyes widened. "Are you... are you sure?"

"We need a place to rest," Keira said. Barely able to speak anymore, the exhaustion was so strong. "Nisha... She needs... she needs help."

Kevin nodded. And Keira knew things were going to be complicated. She knew they were going to be difficult to explain. The bite on Nisha's leg. She hoped she'd be able to get away without explaining that at all.

But the question was going to be asked at some stage.

And when it was... Fuck, Keira just didn't have the answers right now.

But then Kevin smiled just a little. "Good," he said, nodding. "Well... welcome to camp, I suppose."

He lifted a hand. Whistled. Waved, some kind of signal.

The gates started rolling open. Screeching into the night.

Keira stared into the camp.

She tasted a sickness on her lips.

She thought about Dad.

She thought about Sarah.

And she thought about Nisha. Right here in her arms.

"Are you sure about this?" Kevin asked. "I don't want you to feel any pressure. I know there's bad people out there. And I don't want you to feel forced into this in any way."

Keira gulped again.

She took a deep breath.

She looked over her shoulder.

Back in the direction they'd left Sarah behind.

"I'm sorry," she said.

And then she took another deep breath.

She turned around.

And she stepped beyond the gates into the camp.

The gates screeched shut.

And then they slammed shut right behind her.

SARAH

* * *

Sarah watched the infected man hurtle towards her.

Keira ran away with Nisha and the military people. And Sarah could only stand there. She didn't have the time to feel any sort of frustration. Or any sort of sadness.

Her priority?

Seeing Keira get away.

Seeing Nisha get away.

Seeing Rufus get away.

To Sarah, their escape was the most important thing. And she really meant that. She never thought she'd ever reach a point in her life where she valued the lives of others over her own.

But that moment was now.

The infected man launched at her. He was a chubby guy, wearing a torn white shirt and leather jacket. Bitemarks covered him. Weeping wounds seeped blood and pus. Some of those wounds were so deep she could see his skull underneath. Fuck. Looked painful. Looked sore. Kind of felt rather sorry for the guy. Had a lot of sympathy for him.

But that sympathy didn't last long.

Not the way he was throwing himself towards her.

She heard more groans from behind. She didn't want to look back. She didn't *have* to look back to know what was coming. Who was coming. The infected. They were approaching. They were surrounding her. They were going to get her. They were going to get her, and there was no way out.

"Sarah!" Keira's voice. Echoing in the distance. Getting further away. So she was leaving her here. And she figured it showed how much she'd grown over the last few weeks that it didn't even bother Sarah all that much. Quite the opposite, in fact.

She was pleased. In a terrified kind of way, she was pleased that Keira was getting away. She was pleased that Nisha was getting away. And she was pleased that Rufus was getting away, too. She liked Rufus. He was absolutely the best dog she'd ever encountered. And it wasn't even a close contest.

Granted, she never really liked dogs before. So the bar wasn't ridiculously high.

But still. A nice sentiment, right?

And in a way, the thought sparked a sadness within. It made her eyes well up with tears. She'd never been one for pets. But at the very end, Rufus was the one to make her realise that perhaps she just hadn't been opening herself up to them quite enough. And that was just so her, wasn't it?

But now she was going to die. And she would never have a chance to bond with another animal again. Another dog again.

Or anyone again.

She smelled the earthiness clawing up her nostrils. Sour now. Sourer than usual. She felt the familiar pain splitting right through her body.

And she watched that infected man inch closer...

She thought of Dad.

She thought of the last time she'd ever seen him. What he said to her. Something she didn't think anything of at the time. But something that always stuck with her.

"You trust yourself, Sarah. Always. You're far wiser than you'll ever know. And you're far stronger than you'll ever know."

She remembered his words, and immediately, the sense of defeat building inside her vanished in a puff of smoke.

No.

No, she wasn't going to give up.

She wasn't going to stand here and give up. This wasn't like childhood again. Lying on the ground as Harry stroked the insides of her thighs, as he touched her while she lay there, defenceless.

It wasn't like adulthood, either. Like Dean. Locking her in that cupboard. Telling her it was for her own good.

She felt like she was right back there. Defenceless. Weak. No way out.

But no.

That wasn't the case.

That wasn't the case at all.

That wasn't how it was going to be.

That wasn't how it had to be.

Things were going to be different now.

She watched the infected man inch towards her in slow motion when suddenly, she saw that long piece of wood—that fallen chunk of tree—right at her feet.

She wasn't on the ground by that tall wall, staring up at Harry.

And she wasn't locked in the cupboard, awaiting Dean's return.

She wasn't defined by her past.

She was Sarah.

She was her father's daughter.

And she was free.

She reached down, and she grabbed the log.

And then she swung it at the infected man's head.

Hard.

The piece of wood cracked in an instant. It split into pieces.

But the piece of wood wasn't the only thing that split.

The infected man's head. Blood splattered out of it. Splashed all over the place.

And the infected behind Sarah inched closer.

She dropped the piece of wood. And she ran over the infected man's wincing, twitching, screaming body. She had to get to the road. She had to get to Keira. She had to...

More movement.

Movement up ahead.

Silhouettes.

Gasps.

And...

Wait. Was that...

A shriek. Like a screaming child. Wailing. And... and crying *words* under its breath: "Please, Daddy. Don't bite me. Please."

And hearing this sound, it had an almost echoey quality to it. Like it wasn't really happening. Like it wasn't real at all. And it sent a shiver down Sarah's spine.

What was this?

What was happening?

She listened to that screaming, that begging, as the hairs on her arms stood on end. And she realised what it was. It was one of the infected. Somehow, it was making the sound of a shrieking, begging child. Almost like someone pleading for someone not to kill them.

A shiver crept down her spine. More gasps behind her. Edging closer.

And that movement.

Getting closer up ahead.

Blocking her way towards Keira and the rest of that group.

She looked back, and she realised she had no way out here.

She was trapped.

But...

No.

She wasn't trapped.

She wasn't giving up.

She looked to her right. Saw a tree. A tall tree. A few branches jutting out of it. Solid-looking branches. And even if it'd been years since she'd climbed a tree, she used to love doing that as a kid. So maybe that could work. Maybe that was her way out.

She raced towards the tree as the infected ran towards her from either side.

Their shrieks getting louder.

The smell of their decay mixing with the smell of her own sweat.

Come on, Sarah. You can do this. You can do this.

She ran towards the tree.

She ran towards it, and she was lying on her back as a child again, trying to get to her feet.

She was trapped in the cupboard again, banging against the door, trying to break free.

You can do this.

You can do this...

The shrieks got louder.

The smell surrounded her.

The figures got closer.

The pain in her body intensified.

"You can do this," she gasped. "You can..."

And then she slammed against the tree.

Grabbed a branch.

Yanked herself up onto it and dragged herself up it, up towards the darkness, up towards the rain, as beneath her, the infected cried, they screamed, and one of them shrieked, like a terrified child...

"Don't let me die, Daddy," it gasped in that uncanny, alien, slightly *off* manner. "Don't hurt me..."

And all Sarah could do was perch there, clinging onto that flimsy tree branch in the darkness and pouring rain.

Surrounded by echoes.

Surrounded by groans.

Surrounded by violence.

Alone.

KEIRA

* * *

Keira sat in the dark confines of the old bunker, and for the first time in as long as she could remember, she took a deep breath and let something resembling relaxation seep into her body.

But with the relaxation came the pain.

The pain of loss.

Of Dad.

Of Sarah.

It was dark in here. Very dark. The bunker itself wasn't like she expected inside. She pictured it to be like one of those abandoned places that urban explorers lost themselves in and took photos of. And perhaps once upon a time, it was like that.

But right now, it wasn't like that.

It wasn't like that at all.

There were computers everywhere. Old CRT monitors and big computer boxes. Real old equipment, old tech.

The air smelled metallic. Rusty. And there was a shitload of dust in here, too, catching on Keira's chest. She could hear the rumble of voices all around her. She could hear footsteps banging against the old metal flooring.

A bitterness crossed her lips. That same bitterness that always accompanied her when she was exhausted. Her body ached. Her body was weak. So weak. She wanted to pass out. She wanted to fall asleep. She wanted to sleep for weeks. She felt like if she closed her eyes, she might drift straight off, pass out, and not wake up again for God knows how long.

And that worried her. It panicked her.

Because she still didn't know what this place was. Not truly.

Not well enough to doze off. Not well enough to risk sleeping.

And if she *did* sleep, she feared what she might see in her dreams.

Sarah.

Sarah, standing there, down that bridleway. In the middle of a mass of infected.

Staring back at her with wide, terrified eyes.

And then the infected swarming her.

"Go."

The resignation in her voice. On her face.

Or Dad.

Looking at her with tears of blood spilling down his face.

Smiling at her.

Gasping, and then...

Turning. Turning into one of the infected. As much as she wanted to deny it. As much as she wanted to resist it.

Turning.

And then the knife.

And then...

She gulped. A coldness clawed up her throat. She still felt in a haze. In a dream. Like everything that'd unfolded wasn't actually real. Because it couldn't be real. Maybe it was the way the mind protected itself from trauma. Keira should know. She'd been through enough.

But she knew the shock would hit her eventually. It'd catch up with her. It'd pursue her. Chase her down.

And then it would hit her with all its brutal, devastating force.

She looked around. Saw Nisha lying there, right by her side. She was still out. Still unconscious. But she looked like she was twitching a bit more now. Like her eyes were twitching and moving beneath her eyelids. Now and then, she let out a little mumble, too. A little sign of life. Like she was dreaming. Like she was trapped in a dream, and she was trying to break out of it, trying to wake up from it.

Keira held her hand. Stroked it. Softly. Rufus lay there by her side, snoring.

"You'll be okay," Keira said. "You're going to be okay. I promise."

She looked around. She was in a private little room. Old computers. Old instructions that Keira didn't understand painted the walls, crisping and folding at the corners. Looked another language. Russian, perhaps. Obviously some relic from when this place actually *was* a bunker.

The guy, Kevin. He seemed like he was some sort of authority figure in this place. Which was... jarring, to say the least. She hadn't encountered any sort of real authority figure for weeks now. The police collapsed on day one. And there were no real military figures around, at least not around Preston, anyway. Sarah mentioned a dodgy military group, which made her worry about trusting these people a bit.

But Kevin. He seemed... genuine. And there were other people here, too. People like her and Nisha. From the little he'd told her, they were just a small military group who had fled an overrun barracks and then spent the following days and weeks trying to restore a sense of order. To try and provide as many people as possible with a place of safety. Of respite.

He'd told her all these things as they made their way towards this little private room on this old, Soviet-style corridor.

She'd seen people in the rooms. Military men and women looking at her, smiling at her.

And normal people, too. Women holding babies to their breasts. Men sitting beside their pale-faced children, who rested their heads on their shoulders. A little boy in Pokemon pajamas, smiling and waving at her. A rare moment of friendliness in a world of pain.

And it was all... overwhelming. It was all a lot. And Kevin seemed to get that. He seemed to understand it.

He just wanted them to get some rest.

And she respected that.

She held Nisha's hand. Held it, stroked it softly. And as she sat holding on to Nisha's hand, it struck her that she hadn't had time to process what had happened to Dad yet. Not even slightly. She hadn't had the time to let it sink in. She hadn't had the time to really think about it.

Just the shock.

The shock of being there beside him.

Of watching his eyes turn red.

Of watching the blood ooze from his lips.

Of watching him grow more and more desperate, less and less like himself, and then...

The knife.

Through his chest.

That gargled gasp.

And then a smile across his face.

And silence.

Tears welled up behind her eyelids. It wasn't that she wasn't privy to the horrors this new world might throw her way. She knew to expect the worst from any given situation. The infected were ruthless. And no one was immune to their assault. Even Nisha, who had shown some degree of resistance... something else was going on with her now. Something different entirely.

She looked at Nisha, lying there, silent. Shaking. Twitching.

Teeth clicking together in this unconsciousness. She wondered what she was seeing. What she was witnessing in her dreams. She wanted to reach in and comfort her. Reassure her she was okay. Everything was going to be okay.

She'd asked Kevin what they could do with her from a medical perspective. And he'd told her, with a grim look, that the best thing she could do right now was rest. Rest? That was the solution? That was the answer from authority figures about how to handle the sick, now?

But then... what else could she do?

What else could anyone do?

She squeezed Nisha's hand a little tighter. "We'll get you right again," she said. "I'll look after you. I'll protect you. I promise." Even though Nisha couldn't hear her, she hoped the comfort would seep through.

She thought of Dad.

Sitting amidst the grass, blowing in the breeze.

That smile on his face.

That contented smile, which somehow grew more pronounced the further she walked away from him.

Happy.

At peace.

And then she thought of the fear on Sarah's face.

Sarah.

Sarah, urging her to go.

Urging her to run.

And Keira... not *wanting* to go.

Not *wanting* to run.

Because for a moment, as she stood there on that bridleway, Nisha in her arms... she wanted to join Dad.

She wanted it all to end.

Every last bit of it.

She stroked Nisha's hand. She couldn't think like that

anymore. She had to stay strong. No matter how shocked she was. No matter how much horror she faced.

She had a duty to Nisha.

And she intended to fulfil that duty.

Suddenly, a door creaked open.

She looked around. It was Kevin. He half-smiled at her. Nodded. Glanced at Nisha, then back at Keira. A cacophony of chatter followed him from the dusty, candle-lit corridor into this private room. A flutter of life. Of hope.

"Just thought I'd check on you two," Kevin said. "Or three. Not forgetting the pup. Sorry to intrude. If you were sleeping, I can—"

"Don't worry," Keira said, shaking her head. "I don't imagine I'll be getting much sleep."

Kevin walked further into the room. "You should. You need rest. We all need rest. And... and we need to savour the moments when we get a chance *to* rest. Lucky for you, this is your opportunity."

"I don't feel particularly lucky right now."

"Sorry. I didn't mean to make light of what you're going through. How is she?"

Keira looked around at Nisha. "No change. Perhaps a little more conscious. I'm not sure. It's hard to tell."

"I wish we could do more for her. But you have to understand our situation here."

"You told me to rest and that you would elaborate on your situation later. Which is it?"

Kevin opened his mouth. Then he sighed. Shook his head. "I'm sorry. I was just trying to figure out what might be best for you. But if you want to know..."

"I think it might help."

Kevin leaned against the wall. Folded his big arms around his chest. Stared into the candle-lit darkness. "We were stationed just a few miles from here. At a local barracks. We didn't get any warning about the outbreak. Sure, there were riots and talks of attacks across a few of the big cities. We were on hold in case we needed to be called in. But it all seemed so alien. So far away. You know?"

He gulped. Peered into space.

"The first we saw of the virus? Two of our own. Breaking out of their digs. Attacking people in the common room." He shook his head. "I'll never forget the screams. Walking in. Seeing one of my friends, Harvey. On the floor. Straddling... straddling a guy called Brett. I thought there was funny business going on at first. Couldn't fucking get my head around it. But when I looked closer... I saw the blood. I saw the blood spurting up from his neck, all over Harvey's face. Splattering all over the floor around. People running. People going crazy. Screaming. Like a nightmare. Like I was witnessing something on television. From outside my body. I couldn't make sense of it. Couldn't process it. We train for the worst of situations. For, like, the most grisly combat. But this... this just froze me."

A knot tightened in Keira's stomach. Just hearing these stories brought the horrors of the hospital on day one rushing right back. She'd been through different situations. But the horror... the horror was just the same.

"We wanted to quarantine them. Tried to call the emergency services. But that was in chaos. Couldn't get through. And then... and then others started changing. The people who'd been bit. They started *attacking* our people, too. No justification. No warning. Just... violence. Pure, contagious violence."

He wiped his eyes. Looked like he was tearing up a bit.

"What did you do with the infected?" Keira asked.

He looked around at Keira. Right into her eyes. "The barracks. Our outpost. It isn't standing anymore. You probably saw the flames for miles. But we couldn't stay there. Not with it compromised."

"I'm sorry you had to go through that."

Kevin nodded. "It was panic after that. Some of our people went home. Or tried, anyway. But others... We aren't lucky enough to have homes. Not the sort our friends were going back to, anyway. So we stayed together. Stuck together. Moved from place to place. And after a week or so, we found ourselves here."

Keira looked around at the dark, dusty walls. A shiver crept down her spine.

"I know it's not much. But it's safe. And we've been able to help people. We've been able to bring people inside." He paused. Just for a moment. "And there's something else, too. Something you should know about."

Keira frowned. "What?"

Kevin reached into his pocket. He pulled out a small tape recorder. Held his thumb over it. Then hit "play."

A fuzzy recording echoed through the recorder. It was almost impossible to figure out what was being muttered on there.

"I can't hear anything."

Kevin raised a finger. "Listen," he said.

Crackly static continued to emit from the tape recorder. A knot tightened in Keira's stomach. Had he gone mad? Had the best part of a month trapped in this hellhole sent him loopy? She tightened her grip around Nisha's hand. She had to be ready to run. She had to be ready to get out of here. She had to stay on her toes at all times.

And then, out of nowhere, she heard it.

Her stomach tensed up. But not with fear. With something else entirely.

With something that felt like... optimism.

Because she could hear something on this tape recorder.

Something *clear*.

"You see?" Kevin said. "You understand now?"

Keira's heart raced.

Her stomach tensed.

A smile tugged at the corners of her lips as she held onto Nisha's hand.

She understood.

And she understood clearly.

Because those words.

Those words on the tape recorder.

Those words had the potential to change everything.

SARAH

* * *

Sarah sat on the creaky tree branch and prayed to God it was strong enough to support her.

If indeed there *was* a God. Which, to be honest, she very much doubted because it went against the rules of logic.

But anyway. The presence or non-presence of an omniscient god wasn't her greatest concern right now.

Her greatest concern?

The infected gathered right underneath her.

Their groans growing louder.

The nightmare in this pitch-black night, unending.

She stared up at the sky as the rain hammered down from above. She tried to focus on the stars. If she focused on one thing intently enough, she could ignore the rest of her surroundings. She could make the rest of the world fade away. She'd learned that in a trauma course she went on when she was younger. She hadn't lasted long. The trauma was, as it turned out, too much to deal with.

But there was something that stuck with her from those brief conversations.

Meditation. Mindful focus. She thought it sounded a bit hokey at first. A bit far-fetched. Spiritual bullshit.

But when the memories were strong, when the flashbacks were intense, she found herself sinking into that concentration state more and more.

Focusing on her breath.

Following her breathing at the expense of everything else.

Or watching the flame of a candle flickering away.

She found herself sinking into that focus. Sinking into the flickering flame. Or into her breathing. And the trauma, sinking away, disappearing. The memories of Dean. The memories of Harry. All of them... drifting, and...

A groan echoed up the side of the tree she was on. And the tree began to shake, too, immediately jolting her out of the present. She looked down, even though she knew it was a bad idea right away. She saw one of the infected, a big bloke in a torn white T-shirt, shaking the side of the tree. Screaming. Groaning. Punching the wood with his fists. Fuck. The tree was going to break. She was going to fall. Fall to her death.

The smell of damp earth flooded her nostrils. There was something else to that smell, too. Something she hadn't noticed before. Something she couldn't quite put her finger on initially. But there was a kind of medicinal quality to it. And a *familiarity* to it.

Almost like... like it was nostalgic. The first thing she'd ever smelled. The first thing she'd ever experienced. It was *that* level of familiarity.

And yet, it was the most *alien* thing Sarah had ever encountered, all at the same time.

Mother.

She shuddered. That thought. That word. She had no idea where it came from.

But it made her feel uneasy.

Really fucking uneasy.

She perched there on that creaking tree branch. Fucking great idea, crawling her way up here, hiding up here. What was she going to do now? The infected weren't going to get bored. They had some easy prey right here, waiting for them. She was going to fall off the branch. She was going to fall off the branch and down to her death, and the infected were going to rip her apart.

But what the hell else was she supposed to do?

She was trapped up here. And there was no way out.

So what on Earth could she do?

She looked down at the infected. Saw them all gathered around the tree. Staring up at her with those blank, bloodshot eyes. Screaming.

And there was something else, too.

Something that turned her stomach.

Something that jolted her even further out of any semblance of presence and right back into the horror of her surroundings.

One of the infected. A man. No, barely a man. A teenage boy, by the looks of things. Dark hair. Kind of an emo fringe, if an "emo fringe" was indeed still a thing. Wearing all black, with a band T-shirt.

He was looking right up at Sarah.

And...

And he was doing something else, too.

Something that sent shivers down her spine.

The boy.

He was... *whining*.

Like a baby.

He looked up at her with clarity. With a much more perfect clarity than the rest of the infected here. Almost like he was more present. Almost like he was more... *tuned in*.

But the noise he was making.

The sound.

A screaming child.

A screaming baby.

In agony…

A splitting, sickening bolt shot through Sarah's body. That crying. That screaming. The groaning was bad enough. The sounds of the infected were always bad enough.

But this…

This was something entirely different.

Just like the man before. The way he begged.

The infected. It was almost as if they were adapting.

Changing.

How far did that go?

How far did they evolve?

She pictured being surrounded by the infected for hours on end. Trapped in the midst of them. Those groans. They would be enough to drive anyone crazy.

But these agonised sounds…

They were far, far worse.

She sat on the tree branch, clinging tightly, and looked around for some kind of escape. But she didn't see any. If she tried to climb across the branch, she'd just end up being followed by the infected. If she stayed here, she would fall into the mass of infected eventually. This branch wasn't gonna hold forever. She was gonna get thirsty. Hungry. She was gonna doze off and collapse.

What did she do? She had to do *something*.

But what?

What could she do?

She took a deep breath. Tried to focus on her breathing. Keira. She'd watched Keira walk away with those military guys. She'd watched them closely. And she didn't trust them. Not after what she'd been through on the road.

But at the same time, those men. They'd gunned down the infected. They'd *helped* them.

So, who was to say they weren't trustworthy?

Gosh, Sarah didn't know. She didn't have a clue. She wasn't sure at all.

But she could only take what she'd witnessed at face value.

Those people had helped.

Those people had—

A crack.

A crack that sent a shiver down her spine.

No. No, it couldn't be what she thought it was. It just couldn't.

She looked down.

Slowly.

And she saw it.

The branch. The branch she was sitting on.

It was cracking.

It was bending.

The wood underneath the bark was revealing itself as the branch slowly bent.

And the infected were gathered around the base of the tree.

Waiting for her to fall.

Sarah's stomach turned. Her chest tightened. No. No, this couldn't be it. It couldn't be a fall that killed her. It felt like falls had defined her entire life.

The wall.

The supermarket.

And now...

The branch cracked some more.

The chorus of infected cries echoed louder, up towards the top of the tree, in the darkness, in the falling rain.

She looked up. The other side of the tree. The other branch.

She had to get there.

And she had to get there fast.

She took a deep breath.

Then she scrambled across the branch. Towards the next branch.

She was going to be okay.

Everything was going to be okay.

She clambered across the falling branch to the next branch when suddenly, she felt something that made her stomach sink.

Made her whole damned body sink.

The branch beneath her.

It split some more.

Shifted.

And then…

Sarah held her breath.

Please no. Please, please, no.

The branch snapped.

And suddenly, Sarah was floating.

For a second, floating.

Engulfed in fear, Sarah couldn't help contemplating the poetic irony. It was just typical, wasn't it?

A life defined by falls.

And a looming death defined by a fall.

She hovered.

Hovered in mid-air.

Heart racing.

Stomach sinking.

Frozen.

And then, inevitably… she fell.

Fell towards the ground.

Fell towards the infected below.

Fell towards her inevitable fate.

KEIRA

* * *

Keira heard the crackling voice on the tape recorder, and suddenly, everything changed.

She sat there in the darkness of this private room in the bunker, holding Nisha's soft, warm hand. She could hear the rain outside, hammering down, hitting the metal bunker roof. Kevin stood opposite her in his military greens, holding that tape recorder in his hand. He smelled of sweat and gasoline.

And that voice.

On the tape recorder.

It stopped. And then he rewound it. Played it again. Just to confirm its reality to Keira.

She sat there. Frozen. Her heart raced. What did it mean? It sounded pretty clear what it meant. It sounded pretty obvious from those words. But it was just so hard to comprehend. After so many weeks of loss... it was just so hard to *believe*.

But those words. Crackling away.

They filled Keira with hope.

Even though she'd learned to take things with a pinch of salt, they filled her with hope.

Kevin looked right at her. "What do you think?"

She shook her head. What did she say? How was she supposed to process that? Especially so soon after losing Dad. So soon after losing Sarah. Losses that she still hadn't even begun to process. She knew the time to process them would come. She knew the time to grieve would come. The time to mourn would come.

But that time wasn't now.

"Are you sure about it?" Keira said.

Kevin lifted his thumb. Rewound the tape again. "Sure as I can be."

"Where did this come from?"

"One of the old comms systems in the back. Before the power went out. This place. It was some sort of surveillance place. The backup generator coughed along for a good couple of weeks. We stayed connected, kept on checking, just in case. Lost all hope. And then this comes through. This evening. Right before the system packed in completely."

Keira shook her head. It seemed too good to be true. And yet... here it was. Right in front of her.

"Play it again," Keira said.

Kevin nodded.

He held his thumb over the play button.

And then, he pushed the button.

First, the blast of static. The interference. The muffled sounds in the background.

And then...

Voices.

Clear voices.

"If anyone can hear this, we're stationed at the North Lancashire barracks. We have plenty of food. We have hundreds of people here. We have walls. Fresh water. Warmth. Supplies. Medical supplies. We have everything. It's safe here."

And this alone—this alone was enough to fill Keira with some kind of confidence. Some kind of hope. First, the authority figure in the form of this smaller military group, seemingly headed by Kevin.

And now, talk of a larger group. A safe place. A real, promising, safe place.

The group with the helicopter. Could this be something to do with them? Because it certainly wasn't anything to do with Kevin's group. Kevin's group had numbers, and it had some supplies. But helicopters were a whole different level entirely.

But it was what the voice said afterwards that really stood out to her.

That really changed everything.

"I know this may sound far-fetched. I know this may sound alien. But we have... we have a way of stopping the infected. We have a way of... an antidote to..."

And then the voice fizzled off into static.

A few more muffled words.

Something about: "Codeword. Bracken Cave. You need..."

More static.

Then, nothing.

Keira sat there. Heart racing. The excitement she felt right now. It was unmatched. It was unlike anything she'd felt for a long, long time. It was dampened. Dampened by the loss of Dad. Dampened by the loss of Sarah. And dampened by Nisha's condition.

But... this talk.

This talk of a safe place of some kind.

And some whispers of an *antidote*...

"Did he definitely say 'antidote'?" Keira asked.

Kevin shrugged. "What did you hear?"

Keira brushed her fingers through her greasy hair. "It sounded like 'antidote'."

"Then I'd say it's pretty likely that's what he said, wouldn't you?"

She looked down at Nisha. Rufus still lying there, right by her side. She knew what Nisha was capable of. She knew how she could repel the infected. And she knew that she was immune.

But something was changing in her.

Something was *different* about her.

She pulled the fabric of her trousers down, making sure her bite mark was definitely covered.

Because while she trusted her first impression of Kevin... she didn't know whether she could fully trust him or his people with *that* sort of information just yet.

"I heard rumours," Keira said. "On the road. About some military place. Who had a girl. I thought it might be you at first."

Kevin nodded. "It makes sense. If you've heard of them, too... then maybe they are for real. Maybe they are the people with the helicopter you spoke of."

He paused. Muttered under his breath. Like he was trying to piece together the jigsaw. Connect the dots in his head.

"This place," Kevin said. "The talk of supplies. Medical supplies. Maybe they can help her."

Keira nodded. "North Lancs. How far a journey are we talking?"

"A good few days. Maybe a week on foot."

"You have vehicles."

"But not enough gas," Kevin said. "And besides. Vehicles draw attention. From the infected. And from... other people."

Keira took a deep breath. Nodded. It kind of made sense.

"We're establishing a small group to set off in the morning. To establish the safety of this place. Seeing as the girl needs help... I wondered if you wanted to join. But I can understand if you want to assess the situation first. Wait for our findings."

Keira felt torn. She looked at Nisha. Her paling face. Her

twitching eyes. She heard her gasping breaths. And saw the dried blood around her nostrils, around her lips. She didn't know how much time Nisha had left. If she stayed here, right here, then something might happen to her. And she'd never forgive herself for not trying, especially when an opportunity opened up right in front of her.

Especially with whispers of hope.

"I understand if you want to stay here," Kevin said. "It's safe here. There's good people here. We have supplies, like I said. Not an awful load. But enough. But these supplies. They are stretched. And they... they will run out. Not just now. But they will run out. Especially as we grow. And that's something we have to deal with. But this place. If it's as the bloke says it is... this could be our chance. If they have hundreds... then there must be real order there. Safety. Real safety for our people."

Scepticism crawled through Keira's skin. Where hope would've prevailed so recently... scepticism.

But she knew why it was.

It was a defence mechanism.

"I don't want to get too hopeful," Keira said. "Because I don't think I can face any more loss."

Kevin nodded. "Then I understand if you—"

"But I can't pass this opportunity up," Keira said.

Kevin looked back up at her. His eyes widened.

"For Nisha. I can't just sit here. I can't just wait around. I made a promise. And I intend to keep that promise."

She gulped down a lump in her throat.

She took a deep breath as exhaustion crept through her every muscle.

And then, with Nisha's unconscious, twitching hand in hers, she stood.

"I'll join the group," Keira said. "We'll find this place. And we'll get Nisha to safety. We'll get your people to safety. No matter what it takes."

NISHA

* * *

Nisha was with the girl again.
She saw her clearly now. Her long brown hair. Her pale face. Those marble eyes. They looked green now. Burning green.

Which was a weird thing to think because green eyes weren't burning like fire. Green eyes were more peaceful. Like emeralds. Whatever emeralds were. She'd read the word once, and she thought it sounded nice. She imagined emeralds to be like diamonds, only maybe even nicer. Shinier. A nicer glow.

The girl sat opposite her. She was in some kind of room. At first, she thought it was a big room, spacious. But now she wasn't sure. She could see the room better now. It was smaller. Cramped. Like a cupboard or a closet under the stairs.

Nisha got stuck in a closet under the stairs once. She was only very little. She was around at Dad's weird brother's place. He was called Hassan. Nisha never liked Hassan because he used to smell funny and he used to speak to her with a smile even though he knew she couldn't hear, and then he'd turn around and laugh, and

Nisha would feel like she was at school again, and she was missing out on the joke.

But this felt different.

In here, with this girl, she felt safe, somehow.

She looked down and realised she was in a body. Not hovering in the air. She was in a body. Only... this body was chained up. There were chains around the wrists. And around the ankles. And she could feel a chain around her belly, too. And she realised she was in the head of a bad person again. Only...

This girl.

The girl opposite her.

She didn't look scared.

She didn't look afraid.

She just looked right at the bad person—right at *Nisha*.

And this was different from when she last saw this girl. Because last time, she felt like she wasn't in a body at all. She was... floating. She was floating, and in a place only she and the girl could speak. It felt nice. It felt warm. It felt...

Like home.

Like she was *understood*.

The girl with the emerald eyes looked at the bad person. Or maybe she was looking through the bad person's eyes and at *her*. Maybe she could see Nisha. Because Nisha didn't understand it. She didn't understand any of it. She just knew that there was something with a voice in her head, and then there was something with her going into the bodies of the bad people, and there was something with—

Suddenly, she was there again.

In the dark.

In the nice, warm dark, with only her and the girl.

The girl opened her lips.

And this time, a sound came out.

Once again, a sound came out.

A sound that, somehow, she *understood*.

But it was different to last time.

And it was as if it was happening in her head. Right in her head.

Find me. We can help other people.

We can be together.

These words in her head. Were they the words of the girl? Or were they the words of that... *other voice?*

The voice that was like the words she saw in her own head when she was thinking.

But the voice that was *different*, somehow.

Different to her.

Becoming her.

You are us my dear you are us you join us you take us to good people good souls we give you everything we give you—

That sound.

That's what it was. A *sound*.

In her head again.

Splitting again.

And suddenly, she was lying on her back in some dark room, and Keira was above her, holding her hand, and her mouth was moving, and she was talking to her. Talking to her but also talking to some other man. A man in the same green as the bad men on the road.

The ones who tried to hurt her and Sarah.

And Rufus was by her side.

She tried to move her lips. She tried to say something. She tried to squeeze Keira's hand. She wanted her to know she was okay. Because what if she fell asleep and they thought she was dead? Dad told her that happened to someone at work once. A little boy. He was in an accident, and someone turned his "life machine" off. What if someone turned Nisha's life machine off? She didn't want that. She didn't want that because she was alive. She was wide awake.

She tried to prise her eyes open. She tried to open her mouth. She tried to move her hand.

But the darkness.

It just kept coming.

It just kept surrounding her.

Like a curtain.

Wrapping itself around her.

Covering her face.

Covering her eyes.

And...

Silence.

Darkness.

And then...

It's time, my dear.

It's time.

She felt her tummy go all weird. And then she felt like she was running. Trying to run away.

Run away from the voice.

Run away from the voice in her head.

Don't resist Mother.

You are Mother.

And then the girl.

The girl in her head saying those words.

Find me.

She ran through the dark. But she could *feel* the voice. She could *feel* it seeping into her body. She could *feel* it running down the back of her neck. She could *feel* it taking over her. *Becoming* her.

She tried to shake. She tried to break free. She tried to get away.

But she couldn't.

She closed her eyes.

Darkness surrounded her.

But when she opened them, she didn't see darkness.

She didn't see darkness at all.

When she opened her eyes, Nisha saw...

Light.

She saw a corridor.

A long, dark corridor, with candles either side.

With doors right the way down.

Doors with people behind them.

She stood there in the darkness, and she felt that voice deep inside her chest again.

And this time, when it spoke... there was nothing she could do to resist it.

Nothing she could do to fight it.

It's time.

FRANCO

* * *

Franco opened his eyes and gasped.

He launched forward. Sweating. Panting. It was pitch black. But his dreams. His dreams had been... so clear. He dreamed he was walking down a long, dark corridor. He recognised the corridor. It was a corridor he walked down a lot. The smell of cigarette smoke and metal mixed with body odour. A bitter taste of alcohol stretching across his lips. The old Cold War posters on the wall, Soviet ones for good measure. Candles, flickering, lighting up the grey walls. The bunker. He was dreaming he was in the bunker.

And it seemed weird. It wasn't such a memorable dream. He was only walking, after all.

But, weird as it might sound, he couldn't shake the feeling he was walking *towards* himself.

He couldn't shake the sense of dread and also just how *real* it felt.

But he was awake now. He could taste sweat pouring down his cheeks. His nostrils burned. Damn it. Getting a cold. There had been a nasty bug going around the place. Got a bunch of people worried. Course it did. When there was an infection like *that* outside, *any* little sniffle was enough to make people panic.

He reached up to wipe his running nose when he saw something on his fingers.

Blood.

His stomach turned. He felt a little dizzy. He wasn't good with blood. Which, being a soldier, wasn't a good thing. When he joined, he figured he'd never really see any real action anymore. He'd just about missed the Iraq and Afghan years by the time he started. He figured war would be a pretty much an online, cyber thing if he ever faced it.

But seeing this blood on his fingers.

Seeing it dripping from his nostrils.

It made him feel sick.

It made his head feel woozy.

It made him all tingly. Not in a mother-fucking good way, either.

He cleared his throat. Looked around. Saw a couple of other people lying there in the darkness. Fast asleep. Good. That's how he wanted it. He didn't want to be bothering any of his mates with the sight of the blood. It'd drive people crazy. Get him quarantined.

Fraser had come down with some sort of sinus thing a few days back. Bleeding from his nostrils. They shoved him into a room and slid meals under the door for him until they were absolutely certain he wasn't infected. Even though he wasn't, no one was mad keen on sharing a damned room with him. Who would be? They didn't really know a damned thing about how the virus worked or spread. So nobody was volunteering to spend time with a bloke who had symptoms like that. Rightly fucking not, as far as Franco was concerned.

He felt the warm blood in his fingers. Tasted it, metallic in his mouth.

Besides. They didn't want to freak out the civilians. There were quite a few of them here, now. Franco was torn about it. On the one hand, he wanted to help people. On the other, there were only so many supplies to go around. They were going to run out eventually.

And they were going to run out a whole lot quicker with extra mouths to feed.

But hell. He got it.

He felt alright about most civilians except for the new arrivals today.

The woman. The kid. The dog.

There was something about them that gave him the creeps.

The kid in particular.

Unconscious.

But something... different.

Something...

Wrong.

And there was something about that weird dream he'd had that made him feel closer to her and more familiar with her than ever, somehow.

He crept out of bed. Across the hallway, into the night. Just had to head to the bathroom. Just had to get cleaned up. Swill his face, then get back to bed and hopefully get another couple of hours of sleep before being forced to survive another damned day.

He figured he couldn't complain, really. He was lucky. Surviving in this bunker. Locked away from the outside world.

And besides. He'd heard the rumours.

The rumours of sanctuary.

The rumours of safety.

They were gonna head out tomorrow. Get a small group to head that way. They needed it. They sure as shit needed it.

He stepped out of the room he slept in with four others and onto the candlelit hallway.

The flames flickered. Most of them had gone out. It was pitch black. Even with the candles flickering away, it was still pitch black. And there were no windows down here, either. So it was this long, constant night.

His granddad used to tell him tales of when he worked in the pits. He used to tell him tales of the suffocating heat. Of the stench of smoke clinging to his lungs even to his later days. He used to tell him of those tunnels, so narrow he couldn't even stand up properly in. And all the tales of collapsing tunnels, and explosions, and all the like. He used to tell him how terrifying it was back then. But with a sense of weird pride.

But right now, Franco felt like he was down in those pits. In the darkness.

He stared into the darkness. His heart thumped. The dream he'd had. The dream that he was walking down the corridor. That he was walking towards his own room. Towards *himself*.

That dream felt so real. In ways he couldn't even explain.

And just moments ago, moments before he stood up... he was standing right there.

Right there in the darkness.

Blood trickled down Franco's face.

He peered into the dark.

A shiver crept down his spine.

Because even though it was dark, even though it was pitch black, he had a horrible feeling.

A horrible sense.

The sense that someone was standing right there in the darkness.

The sense that someone was watching.

He turned around. And then hurried down the corridor. Towards the bathroom area. Makeshift, but it would have to do. He just had to wash his face with a little of the water they'd gathered from the rain outside. Wash his face, freshen himself up, then get back to bed and never mention a thing of it.

He looked back over his shoulder as he stepped into the bathroom.

Where the candle flickered just moments ago... there was no light.

There was just darkness.

Pure darkness.

But in that darkness, Franco felt a presence.

Watching him.

Watching his every move.

He staggered inside the bathroom when suddenly, a voice filled his head.

You are with us now we have you now we have you we...

A splitting, screeching bolt of static filling his skull. Making it feel like it was going to burst. Explode.

Then, a taste on his lips.

Of blood.

Metallic blood.

Oozing down his nostrils.

Pouring from his frothing lips.

And his ears all clogged up, and *they* were leaking, too.

What was happening?

What the hell was—

He collapsed to his knees.

A bitter pain punched his stomach. Like someone was standing in front of him.

Thumping him.

Hard.

He clutched his stomach. And then he vomited. Vomited all over the floor.

When he looked down at the vomit, his head spinning, his body went cold.

Blood.

A pool of blood.

Lumps of *flesh* swimming in the midst of it.

He looked down at that pool of blood, and he staggered back to his feet. He couldn't move. He couldn't think. He couldn't breathe.

He just had to get away.

He stumbled up to his feet when he saw it.

A figure.

Standing right there.

Staring right at him.

Right there in the darkness.

It's okay now you're with us now you're with us...

A bolt of pain.

Splitting through his body.

The taste of blood filling his mouth, filling his throat, metallic and sharp.

And the bitter, acidic tang of vomit, too.

Vomit, and blood, and...

He fell.

Fell to his knees again.

And this time, as he crouched there, shitting himself, the smell of it surrounding him, piss drenching his trousers and seeping out around his ankles, he looked up at that darkness as every candle flickered out, and as that *presence* grew closer, as it tightened its grip around him, like a—

COLONY OF BATS.

It's okay now.

You're with us now.

We feed now.

A pause.

A moment of clarity.

A moment of peace.

Staring.

Staring into a long, dark, beautiful tunnel.

Tears streaming down his cheeks.

"Mother," he said. "Mother..."

And then his neck jolted back.
Snapped.
Darkness.
Then... earthiness.
And then...
Hunger.

SARAH

* * *

For a moment, Sarah felt herself hovering. Hovering in mid-air. The tree branch snapping beneath her weight. The mass of infected looming large, right beneath her.

And then she was falling.

She saw the world rushing past her. The bright glow of the moonlight. The piercing stars. She saw rain hissing by as she descended. She saw tree branches darting past her vision. She could hear those groans getting closer. Not just groans. Screaming, too. Crying. The cursed sound of that infected kid letting out the most desperate, most *human* noise.

A human in pain.

A human in fear.

That's what it reminded her of.

And it sent a shiver right down her spine.

That earthy smell surrounded her. She felt it filling her nostrils. She felt it filling every inch of her body. Consuming her. Bleeding into her like hot water filling a bath. Almost intoxicating. Reminded her of when she was in a house fire as a kid. Not as dramatic a story as it sounded on the surface. Grandma dropped one of her cigarettes. Caused a blaze in her bedroom. She was okay, and Grandma was okay. They managed to get out of the house without any trouble. And as soon as the fire brigade arrived, they sorted it in no time at all.

But Sarah would never forget that smell.

That strong, ghastly smell and how it choked her. How it filled her nostrils, tightened its grip around her throat, and choked her. Smoke inhalation. It was no joke.

And that's what this reminded her of. Right now, that's what this reminded her of.

The earthy smell growing stronger, filling her nostrils, blocking her sense of smell to any interference, and filling her lungs like tar.

Her stomach. It felt like she was tumbling down the drop on a rollercoaster. She hated rollercoasters. She'd gone on one on a school trip. She wasn't afraid of them. She just found the whole activity rather inane. Sitting strapped to some chunk of metal and climbing to a height before tumbling down a track, all in some vague pursuit of a tingly sensation in the stomach. It all seemed rather inane to Sarah. All seemed rather, well, pointless. Futile.

She felt herself falling, and she was falling off that wall again. She was falling to her defenceless fate again. She was falling to inevitable pain and inevitable humiliation all over again.

Harry.

Harry's cold fingers sliding up her legs.

His wide eyes peering down at her.

That slight trickle of drool right at the side of his mouth.

She closed her eyes as the cacophony of infected cries surrounded her.

She held her breath as her heart raced and pounded.

And then she slammed against the ground.

Hard.

A sharp jolt of pain shot right up her spine from the bottom of her back. She let out a cry and regretted it immediately—she never liked appearing weak or vulnerable, especially in the company of strangers. Call it a defence mechanism, perhaps.

But that pain. That splitting ache reverberating right up her back, filling every single bone in her body with splitting agony. It might be awful. It might be completely debilitating.

But the scary thing?

Sarah knew it was nothing compared to the agonising pain that was going to follow.

She held her breath. Her heart pounded. The infected surrounded her. It was time. There was no way out. There was no escape.

But as she lay there, another thought filled her mind.

A rare, selfless thought.

At least Keira had got away.

At least Nisha had got away.

At least Rufus had got away.

She closed her eyes and stared into the darkness as the tears stung the corners of her eyes when suddenly, she heard something.

A bang.

No.

Not just one bang.

A *series* of bangs.

One bang after another.

And they were coming from... coming from somewhere up ahead.

Somewhere in the distance.

No. Not in the distance.

Close.

Really close.

She opened her eyes.

The infected. The ones surrounding her. They were... falling.

Falling over. One after another. Tumbling to her side. Blood splattering up onto her. Just like before.

And that was her first thought. Keira. And the man she was with. Those military types she was with. They were here. They'd come back for her. The fools hadn't left her. Everything was going to be okay.

She tried to drag herself up to her feet. But the pain. The pain in her back. It was just so strong. It was just so intense. And it was filling her entire body with every little move.

But...

No. She couldn't afford to let the pain get the better of her.

She had to get up.

And she had to take this opportunity.

She didn't know where it was coming from or *who* it was coming from.

But she had to take it.

She staggered to her feet.

And in the distance, beyond the three or four infected still staggering her way, she saw someone.

A figure.

A figure in the darkness.

Holding a gun.

"Quick!" they shouted.

A woman.

Sarah gulped. She tried to move, but moving sent another jolt of pain right up her back. She tried to lift her left foot and wade through the mud, but it just made her waddle from side to side. Almost made her collapse.

She held her ground. She took a deep breath. The groans still getting closer. The smell still getting stronger.

"Come on," she muttered. "You've got this. You can do this. Come on."

She lifted her right foot.

She went to put it down.

Another sharp shot of pain.

Another sickening punch right up her spine.

She stood there. Shaking. Struggling to stay standing.

"Quick!" the woman shouted. "There's not much time."

A gasp, right behind her.

A snarl.

Then another gunshot.

"Hurry!"

She closed her burning eyes.

She tried to focus on her breath.

She lifted her left foot...

An explosion of pain erupted right across her back.

Sarah opened her mouth and let out an involuntary gasp.

Her ears rang with pain.

And then, as much as she tried to stay on her feet, as much as she tried to stay standing, she tumbled down and slammed face first against the muddy ground, as the groans approached her, as the gunfire rattled, and as the ringing in her ears grew louder, and the darkness surrounded her, and...

KEIRA

* * *

When Keira opened her eyes, she noticed something was wrong almost immediately.

Her hand. Her hand was cold. It wasn't cold when she... Wait. Dozed off? Shit. She must've dozed off. Dozed off into a dreamless sleep.

The last thing she could remember?

Holding Nisha's hand.

Holding Nisha's hand and stroking the back of it.

Telling her everything was going to be okay. That she was here for her. Right here for her. And that everything was going to work out. Everything was going to be okay.

But her hand was empty now.

There was nothing in her hand.

Nothing holding her hand at all.

Just coldness.

She turned around in this endless darkness, illuminated only by the smallest of candles. A bitter taste crossed her lips. As did a momentary sense of dread. Just a flicker of dread, but it was there.

The smell.

A faint smell.

But a recognisable smell.

A smell she knew well.

All too well.

The smell of the infected.

She looked around, and she saw her.

Her shoulders sank.

Relief surged through her body.

Nisha.

Sitting right there.

Sitting up. At the edge of her makeshift bed, in this side room in the bunker.

She was sitting up.

She was... awake.

She was fucking *awake*.

Keira stood up immediately. She was awake. Which meant she was okay. She was going to be okay. Everything was going to be okay.

"Nisha," she gasped. She stumbled across the cold, hard floor towards the makeshift bed—which was just a table with a few cushions on it. She reached for Nisha's hands as Rufus sat by her side, wagging his tail. "It's okay," she said. "I'm here. I'm..."

And then she noticed something.

It was dark. So she couldn't see very well. She couldn't see very well at all.

But she could see *enough*.

Enough to know.

Blood.

Blood. Oozing down Nisha's face, from her eyes.

And her eyes...

Her eyes were turned back in her head.

The whites on show.

Glowing.

Bloodshot.

She was shaking. Froth bubbled out her lips, and bloody strings of drool trickled down her chin and dangled from her face. Keira could hear a horrible screeching noise. She didn't know what it was. Not until she saw Nisha's teeth clenched together behind her lips. Grinding her teeth. Clenching and grinding them with such ferocity that it looked and sounded like they might just break. Like nails on a chalkboard.

Biting.

Tearing.

Chewing.

Keira gripped Nisha's hands. Tight. Her hands were solid. Solid as rocks.

"Nisha," she said. "I'm here. You're going to be okay. Everything is going to be okay."

She squeezed Nisha's hands. Stroked them. Beside her, Rufus whimpered, the hackles on his back standing tall.

And Keira didn't know what this was. She didn't know what state Nisha was in. She didn't know how it'd started. And she didn't know how it was going to end. From the elation of finding Nisha awake again—finally—to the fear of seeing her in this state now. It was dizzying.

But she held her hands, and she prayed to whoever the fuck was up there that she was going to be okay.

That everything was going to be okay.

She tightened her grip around her hands and...

Suddenly, Nisha's eyes rolled back into place.

She looked at Keira. Looked right into her eyes. Tears of blood ran down her face. The strings of drool fell from her mouth and onto her lap. And almost in an instant, that earthy smell just... dissipated.

But there was an aliveness to her eyes now.

There was an *awakeness* to her eyes now.

"Nisha?" Keira said.

Nisha opened her mouth.

Blood spluttered out.

She looked like she was trying to speak.

And then, in a sudden, terrified rush, she reached her shaking hands into her pockets. She was looking for something. She was trying to find something. The air was cold. Rufus was still hiding. What was happening? What was she trying to...

And then she signalled.

Signalled... writing.

A pen.

Paper.

She wanted a pen and paper.

Keira got up. Still shaking. Scrambled around the room to find a pen and paper. Shit. Nisha was awake. She was actually awake. And she hadn't even been able to process the euphoria—much like she hadn't been able to process the pain of Dad's death—because now Nisha was demanding a pen and paper, of all things.

She searched further around the room, in the darkness, when suddenly she found a pen. She grabbed an old sheet of paper. Some old poster. She ran over to Nisha, her hand shaking, desperate to see what she was trying to tell her. The poor kid had been out cold for God knows how long. Although... that wasn't completely true, was it? Because she must've been somewhat conscious for the infected to resist her. If that was indeed how it worked.

She handed Nisha the paper. God, this kid. Awake after so long. Wasn't asking for water. Wasn't asking for food. Was straight awake and writing. Jotting away on this piece of paper. What was she trying to tell her?

She scribbled away on that piece of paper. And then she held it out to Keira. And Keira couldn't see. She couldn't make it out. Not properly.

But then she handed her the piece of paper. She put it into her hand.

Keira squinted down at it. Tried to see. Tried to squint at it. Tried to make out the writing on that paper. It was small. And the pen didn't look like it was very strong. It was... faint. It was weak.

She pulled it closer to her face when she saw the words.

Suddenly, the words popped out to her.

And they turned her skin cold.

She looked at those words.

Her heart raced.

Her chest tightened.

A bead of cold sweat trickled right down her face.

Those words.

The words on the paper.

Staring right back at her.

She looked down at them.

Read them again. Just to make sure she was reading the right thing. Just to make sure she wasn't misreading anything.

Her skin went cold.

Her chest tightened up.

She wasn't imagining things.

The words.

She wasn't wrong about them at all.

Right there before her.

She looked up at Nisha.

Saw the horror in her wide, bloodshot eyes.

She opened her mouth to say something back to her, and...

And then she heard something that made her freeze.

A piercing scream.

Outside the door.

Down the corridor.

Inside the bunker.

SARAH

* * *

Sarah opened her eyes.

Darkness. Darkness all around her. Only... no, wait. That wasn't entirely true. It wasn't totally dark. There was a little light flickering from somewhere. Candlelight, by the looks of things.

And she wasn't looking up at the sky. She wasn't looking up at the moon. At the stars. She was looking up at a ceiling. Some sort of ceiling. Some sort of roof.

Where was she?

How had she got here?

What was happening?

A sudden bolt of fear filled her chest and body. Dread. Pure dread.

Because she was on the ground.

She was on the ground, and her body was full of pain, and she'd fallen off a tree, and now she was being surrounded by infected.

They were approaching.

They were getting closer.

They were…

No. She wasn't on the ground anymore. She was on… some kind of hard surface. And sure, her back still hurt. And yes, she could still smell a slight metallic tang to the air—the undeniable smell of blood. But she wasn't outside. And she wasn't surrounded by the infected.

So where was she?

She looked around and saw a woman standing beside her.

She was in a caravan. Some kind of small caravan, by the looks of things. A touring caravan. She was lying on the dining table. This woman, she stood there in the darkness, looking down at her. Holding some kind of gun. Staring at her. Intently.

Sarah felt her body freeze. She felt her stomach turn. This woman. This rifle. She was her prisoner. She was holding her prisoner. She needed to get out of here. She needed to find Keira. Needed to find Nisha. Needed to—

"You caused me a lot of trouble," the woman said.

She walked over to Sarah. She was holding something. Holding it out to Sarah. It took Sarah a few seconds to realise what it was.

A bottle of water.

Sarah gulped. She could do with some water now. Her throat was sore and dry. But she didn't feel keen about blindly trusting a stranger.

"Don't worry," the woman said. "It's clean. Besides. If I'd wanted you dead or something, I'd've left you with the biters."

Sarah supposed the woman had a point. It would be quite the display to go to the lengths she'd gone to—shooting down the infected—only to turn around and poison her with dodgy water now, wouldn't it?

She sipped the water. It was cold. Fresh. Rather delightful. Her sips turned to gulps, and she couldn't stop herself like a dog savaging a piece of chicken. She only stopped when the woman grabbed the bottle and yanked it away from her dry, cracked lips.

"That's enough," the woman said. "You'll make yourself sick. And bottled water's a damned premium supply now. Can't just go racing through it like that."

Sarah cleared her throat. The water, so cold, so fresh, it'd recharged her. It'd filled her with life again.

She tried to get off the table. But moving hurt her back. Sent shooting pains right down her spine.

"You were whinging about that back all the way I was carrying you," the woman said.

Really? Sarah didn't remember that. Besides. She didn't like this woman's tone. She sounded sarcastic. Sarah didn't *do* sarcastic. She found it hard to understand. Hard to interpret.

Even though a lot of people *claimed* she was being sarcastic herself quite a lot of the time. She still didn't know how it worked.

"As much as I'm sure you're eager to get out of here—and I get it, the decor could do with some sprucing up—you really need to take it easy right now."

"I need to find my friends."

"Quite a way to thank me for saving your life."

"Thank you for saving my life," Sarah said. "Now I need to save my friends."

She stepped off the table onto her feet, and immediately, that pain gripped her again, making her stumble forward. She grabbed the counter by the dirty old caravan sink for support. Shit. This pain. She hadn't had it this bad for... God, she couldn't remember how long.

"Seriously," the woman said. Scrambling open a box of some sort of painkiller. "You really need to rest. Take a few painkillers—"

"I'm not taking any tablets."

The woman shrugged. She cracked a tablet in half and then knocked one back with a swig of water. "Suit yourself."

Sarah studied this woman. She found her hard to understand. Hard to read. She wasn't wearing military gear. But she had a gun. What did that mean? Did that make her more nervous or less nervous? She wasn't entirely sure. Just a general, base level of nervous, to be quite frank.

Whoever she was, she supposed she had to be grateful she'd helped her. She had to appreciate she'd most likely saved her life. Dragged her over here, apparently. And rescued her from the infected.

She owed her thanks.

But she owed her nothing else.

Because she had friends. And she had to find those friends.

So she gritted her teeth, and even though the pain was still intense, she stood.

She staggered across the caravan. Towards the door. She reached for the handle with her shaking hand. She was weak. She was in pain. There was nothing she could do to make the pain go away. But she had to get out of here, and she had to find the others.

"You don't even know where you are," the woman said. "You don't know how dangerous it might be out there. And you're just walking away?"

"I'll find my way," Sarah said.

The woman rolled her eyes. "Find your way where? To more loneliness? To somewhere exactly like this? Surrounded by the infected? Only with no one to help you next time."

"I'm looking for my friends."

The woman nodded. Smirked a little. "Ahh. Looking for your friends."

"They... are special." She didn't want to say any more than that about Nisha.

"Of course they are."

"They went away with... with a group. Military group. I need to find them."

The woman puffed her lips out. She shook her head. Laughed a little and rolled her eyes.

"What's so funny?" Sarah asked.

The woman shook her head again. "The military. Right."

"What? What's the problem?"

The woman didn't say a word. She just chuckled again.

Sarah launched across the caravan at her. Squared up to her. "What?" she said. "What do you know?"

The woman looked right up at her with these wide, tired eyes. She smiled.

"Your friends. If they went with the military. Then I'm sorry to say, they're already dead."

KEIRA

* * *

Keira heard the scream, and she froze.

It was pitch black in this room, with Nisha and Rufus inside this bunker. Only the slight flicker of candlelight showed her surroundings. It'd been quiet down here for a bit. She had no idea what time of day it was. It felt like an eternal night. But she was pretty sure it was *actually* night, too. Everything had quietened down. Gone very silent.

And then suddenly, out of nowhere, this shrill cry.

Immediately, Keira's body froze. Her stomach turned. That cry. It was the cry of someone struggling. It was the cry of someone in pain.

It was the cry of someone under attack.

Under attack from the infected?

She looked down at the note. The one Nisha handed her just moments earlier. The one she was so desperate for Keira to read immediately after waking up from whatever unconscious state she'd been in.

She read the words across that page. The words she'd been so reluctant to believe. The words she'd questioned from the moment she first saw them.

There was no questioning them.

There was no denying them.

The words were clear.

I've done something bad.

A shiver crept down Keira's spine again. It sent a whole load of questions surging through her mind. Questions about Nisha. How long had she been awake? What had she supposedly done?

And that scream.

Was that something to do with *her?*

She looked up at Nisha. Saw her staring back at her with those wide eyes. Those wide eyes, dripping with bloody tears.

What had she done?

What was happening?

Another scream, then. A man's scream. A gasp. A bitter cry of pain. Of agony.

Keira crouched there in front of Nisha. A shiver crept right through her body, right across her skin. She needed to go outside. She needed to check on this scream. She needed to see what the hell was happening. Who the hell was in danger.

She turned around, and she went to rush over to the door when Nisha grabbed her hand.

Keira looked down at her. She was peering up at Keira with an unfamiliar look.

A look of *fear*.

A level of fear that she'd never seen in this girl's eyes before.

Pure terror.

"What..." Keira started.

But Nisha just stood there. Shaking her head. She didn't want her to go. The way she was looking at her. That terror in her eyes. She didn't want Keira to take a single step out of this room.

But Keira heard that scream. She heard that cry. And even

though Nisha was deaf... the way her eyes widened, it was as if she could hear those screams, too.

Keira pulled her arm away from Nisha.

Then she stepped outside her room.

She stood in the middle of the dark corridor. The doors either side of this corridor were all closed. Why was nobody else out of their rooms? What the hell was happening here? Was this a dream? A nightmare? Because honestly, it was beginning to feel more like that by the minute.

She looked down the hallway. Into the darkness. It was candlelit earlier. But it looked pitch black now.

The scream had stopped. But make no mistake about it. It came from this direction.

She looked down the long corridor. Into the darkness. She gulped. Right behind her, back in the room, she could hear Rufus growling and Nisha panting. Part of her wanted to take Nisha with her. Because she felt like she might be able to protect her. Not to use her as a shield, but... well, she felt vulnerable right now. Really fucking vulnerable.

But the other part of her wanted Nisha to stay right here.

Because she was worried about what she might find.

She walked down the corridor. Further and further down the corridor. Every step felt like an eternity. Her heart raced. Her head spun. She had to do this. She had to keep walking. She had to keep on walking down this corridor. Into the darkness. She had to keep approaching the scream. She had to keep going. She couldn't turn away.

She took another step when suddenly she heard something.

Right behind her.

A door.

Screeching.

She turned around.

Saw movement.

Shooting right across her field of vision in the darkness.

Her stomach sank even further. Her legs turned to jelly. She'd seen someone. Someone was there. She didn't even know anyone here properly. She hadn't even been properly introduced to anyone by Kevin yet.

And now she was standing here in the middle of this corridor.

Terrified.

She went to swallow a lump in her throat when she heard something else.

It sounded like a damp footstep.

A bare foot.

Slapping against the floor.

A damp, bare foot.

She stood there. Frozen.

She didn't want to turn around.

She didn't want to look.

She didn't want to see.

But she did.

She turned around and stared into the darkness and...

She couldn't see anything. Not properly.

But if she squinted right ahead, she swore she could see the outline of something right ahead in the distance.

And it took her back to the hospital on the first day, in the first hour.

The ambient light flickering in the hospital corridors.

The echoing cries.

The blood smeared across the walls.

She stood there, shaking, remarking on the fact that even though it felt like she'd come so far as a person since that day, even though she'd been through so much, changed so much... she was still terrified. And she was still on her own.

That's when she noticed something.

A door.

A door on her left.

It was open.

Ajar.

And...

In the darkness, she could see something trickling from inside that door.

Something jet black.

Something like...

Blood.

She knew she should turn back. She knew she should turn around and just walk away. Just get out of here. Just leave.

But she found herself walking.

Walking towards that door.

Silence.

Silence surrounding her.

Following her every step.

She stopped at the door. Shaking. Heart racing.

She pushed the door open.

She peeked inside.

When Keira saw what was inside that room, what was behind that door, and what was hiding in the darkness... she felt a familiar emotion.

But it was far stronger, far more intense than she'd ever felt it before.

Fear.

SARAH

* * *

"I'm sorry. But if your friends went away with the military, then they're already dead."

Those words. That smirk on this nameless woman's face as she sat there in this dusty, smelly old caravan. The bitter taste spreading across Sarah's lips. And that sickening punch to her gut making her back and her bones hurt even more.

They were... dead?

What was she talking about?

What did she know?

The woman sipped back a bit more water. Although this time, it was a large swig. She gasped when she finished drinking it. Looked up at Sarah. "What? I'm just being honest."

Sarah didn't think. She couldn't think rationally. Not anymore.

She could only stare at this woman and feel this burning sensation in her chest, muscles, and bones.

She launched at the woman. Grabbed her. Pinned her down against the table, which she'd just woken up from. Pain split through her body. Into her fingers. She could barely even stand.

Fuck. She wasn't as strong as she used to be. She felt weak. She felt broke. She felt—

A kick.

Right against the back of her leg.

And then a punch in the middle of her back, and—

The pain.

That explosion of pain.

Taking over everything.

Taking over every single sense.

She fell to the caravan floor. The woman stood over her. Pointing her gun at her.

"What the fuck do you think you're doing?" she shouted.

Sarah turned over. Fuck. Look how pathetic she was. Look how weak she was. Harry was right. Dean was right. Both of them were right.

"I saved your life," the woman said. "And this is how you repay me? Attacking me in my own caravan?"

"You told me my friends were dead," Sarah gasped. "How the hell did you expect me to react?"

"I'm just telling you the fucking truth," the woman said. "If your friends went off with some military types... they're done. That's just a fact."

Sarah clutched her back. She couldn't move. She could barely breathe. God, the pain was bad. Debilitatingly so.

The woman held her gun to her head. Then she muttered something under her breath. Turned around and lowered the gun. Then held out a hand. "Get back on your feet. As long as you promise you won't go apeshit again."

"I can't make any promises."

"No bother," the woman said. "You're not that hard to deal with anyway."

Sarah shook her head. Annoying as it was, irritating as it was, the woman had a point. She wasn't at her best. Far from it. Splitting headache. Taste of blood in her mouth. Ringing ears. And the smells of damp and dust in this place, all of it was giving her a headache.

"I'm sorry," the woman said. "I probably could've been... more tactful with my words."

"You could."

"The military types. They're bad people. That's all I'm saying. If your friends've gone away with some troops... it's probably not good news."

So less of a concrete answer than Sarah was expecting. Which was probably good news.

"I've run into some bad ones myself. But these didn't seem all that bad."

The woman snorted. Shrugged.

"What?"

"Nothing."

"That's usually what someone says when they have something to say?"

She glanced around at Sarah. "The idea of a 'good military type' in a world like this. A world where they weren't there for us when the nation collapsed. Where they've bolstered their own positions and used their arms and strength and resources to take from the weak. Where they've kidnapped people. Raped people. Yeah. Sure. You trust that they're alright. That your pals have just so happened to find the one good military group around here since day one. But I'll take my chances on the road."

She looked away. Shook her head.

"So what am I supposed to do?" Sarah asked.

The woman looked at her. Narrowed her eyes. "Huh?"

"I'm supposed to just give up on my friends? Especially after what you've told me?"

The woman shrugged. "If you value your fucking life, yeah."

Sarah shook her head. She looked at the caravan door. "Maybe once. But... a lot has changed. These people. They are my friends. I can't leave them."

"Sweet. But whatever. Your funeral."

Sarah gulped. She didn't even know this woman's name. She didn't know who she was. Only that she'd helped her. She'd helped her to her feet. She'd helped her from the infected. When all seemed lost, she was there to pick her up again.

"You're proof," Sarah said.

The woman frowned. "What?"

"You're proof. That there are good people out there. If there weren't... maybe I wouldn't be here anymore."

The woman studied her for a long time. Longer than was comfortable for Sarah. "You're weird. You know that?"

Sarah flushed a little. "I have been told that."

The woman smiled. Shook her head. "I'm Carly."

"Carly," Sarah said. "Sarah."

"Sarah. Basic name for a not-so-basic bitch."

"And Carly's a very classy name."

"You taking the piss out of me, Sassy?"

Sassy.

Not the first time she'd been called that. The first time was Harry. All those years ago.

A shiver crept up her legs.

An unspoken past.

She turned around to the door.

"Look," Carly said. "If you have to go, you have to go. I get it. But just be careful, okay? You ain't in the best nick with that dodgy back of yours. Some real knots in there. And... Well, there's some bad types out there. All I'm saying is, the worst types I've come across? They're the ones in military gear. In police uniforms."

She thought of the man on the road, with the gun to her head.

She thought of the police officer who had Nisha in the early days. Pete.

Carly's logic seemed flimsy. But she had a point.

"Thank you," Sarah said.

Sarah reached for the door handle.

"And Sarah?" Carly said.

"What?"

Carly looked right at Sarah with a different look now. A hard expression to read. She looked... paler. And she didn't look as cocky anymore. She didn't look as confident.

She looked... afraid.

"What?" Sarah asked.

Carly opened her mouth.

Held it open for a few seconds.

And then: "If you come across a military bloke called Leonard... you run. Understand? You just run."

A cold shiver crept down Sarah's spine.

"Leonard," she said. "Why?"

Carly stared at Sarah. But it was more like she was staring *through* her now. Like the infected herself.

"Why?" Sarah asked.

Carly looked at Sarah again.

Refocused.

Took another deep breath.

"Because he's the Devil himself."

KEIRA

* * *

Keira thought she knew fear.

But right now, the way she felt... she wasn't quite sure she'd ever felt fear like this before.

The bunker was pitch black. An endless, eternal night. She saw movement in the corners of her eyes every time she blinked. Figures drifting across her field of vision. And she could hear things, too. Muffled footsteps. In her mind, or for real? She wasn't sure. It was impossible for her to know.

All she knew was that scream she'd heard. That was real.

And the sight in front of her.

The *scene* in front of her.

That was real, too.

There was a bitter smell in the air. The smell of metal. The smell of soil. The smell of... blood. Whatever it was—whether it really was the smell of blood or not or another example of her mind playing tricks—it unsettled her. It made her feel nervous.

Because there was something hiding in this darkness.

Something was wrong.

Very wrong.

She stood there. Heart racing. Knees shaking. And as she stared at the scene in front of her, as she squinted at it in the darkness, she tried to tell herself that this could be a figment of her imagination, too. This could all be a part of her terrified mind. An invention. A creation of her consciousness.

But the more she stood there, the longer she stared into the darkness, the more it became clear that this wasn't in her head at all.

At first glance, nothing was wrong. Nothing at all. Just a bunch of people sleeping in their makeshift beds down here in this dark bunker.

But as Keira looked closer... she saw what was wrong.

Exactly what was wrong.

The trail of blood. It led straight towards... towards one of those beds. Right towards one of those makeshift beds. A woman was lying there. She didn't look military. She looked like one of the civilians. Didn't she see her holding a kid earlier? Stroking his head? Kissing him? Tickling him while he giggled away?

And judging by the scene in front of her, she figured she wouldn't be introduced to anyone soon.

Because blood was dripping from this woman's chest.

The bedding had been torn away from her. The sheets were soaked with blood. A clock ticked somewhere above, echoing through the silence.

But this woman.

She lay there.

Lay on the bed.

Vacant eyes staring out into nothingness.

And she wasn't alone.

There was a man by her side. He was holding his throat. Gasping. Gargling. Grunting. And as Keira stood there, as her skin crawled, as the sense of nausea grew inside her, it was Nisha she thought of.

Not just the fact that she'd left her and Rufus alone in that room. But her words.

The words on that piece of paper.

I've done something bad.

She felt sick. She felt dizzy. Her heart raced. Her head spun.

She'd done something bad.

And now two people were lying here in this room.

Attacked.

Infected?

Impossible to know.

Impossible to tell.

She stood there, and she felt sweat trickling down her forehead. She felt a sense of urgency surrounding her. Almost like the darkness was surrounding her. Swallowing her whole. Threatening to chew her up and spit her out and destroy her, once and for all.

And then she heard it again.

The scream.

The stomach-churning scream.

Right down the corridor.

She turned around. Looked over to the right, where the scream came from.

And all she saw was darkness.

Pure darkness.

No signs that anyone was there.

No signs of life.

Only...

Was that a figure?

Was that someone moving right there in the dark?

Or was this in her head, too?

She stared into the darkness. Into the source of that echoing scream. Where was everyone? Why was she the only one standing? Was this a dream? Was this a nightmare? Was this...

And then she heard something to her left.

In the room.

Something that made her skin crawl.

A gargled groan.

Her stomach turned in knots. Her heart thumped. She didn't want to turn around. She didn't want to look to her left. She didn't want to see what was there. Didn't want to see *who* was there.

But as she stood there, staring into the darkness, Keira had no choice.

She turned around.

Slowly.

The woman. The one who was lying on the bed just moments ago.

She was standing now.

She was standing, and she was staring right at Keira.

Keira's stomach sank. She felt the earth dropping out from underneath her. And in a way, she wished it would. Because anywhere was better than here right now.

She couldn't move.

She didn't *want* to move.

Because if she moved, this woman might chase her.

If she moved, this woman might move, too.

It wasn't logical. It didn't make sense. It was kind of like when you were a kid, and you covered your face in the hope that someone wouldn't notice you, wouldn't see you, just because your eyes were covered.

But this illusion didn't work anymore.

And it especially didn't work with the infected.

She stood there. Shaking. Struggling to breathe. Her heart racing. The woman standing opposite her.

Staring.

Groaning.

She needed to get away from here.

She didn't know what was happening. She didn't know what was going on.

But she needed to get away.

She needed to get Nisha.

She needed to get Rufus.

And then she needed to get out of here.

She needed...

And then, suddenly, a cry.

A shriek.

From this woman's mouth.

And then the game of statues was over.

She launched herself towards Keira.

Threw herself at her.

Eyes dead.

Mouth wide.

Keira went to turn around and run for her fucking life.

She had to get away from here.

She had to run.

She went to turn, went to spin around, went to race away as fast as she could.

And then, suddenly, out of nowhere, she felt something.

A tight squeeze.

Around her right arm.

A hand.

Grabbing her.

Burying its nails deep into her skin.

And dragging her into the darkness.

SARAH

* * *

Sarah stepped out of the caravan and into the woods, and the more she walked, the more hopeful she grew that her agonised back wasn't going to cripple her after all.

It was growing light. Wow. How long had passed since the events of last night? It was impossible to say. Impossible to know. But it all felt so long ago. Losing David. All the shit that unfolded since. It seemed alien. It seemed distant. It seemed like a faint memory. Like a dream.

But it absolutely wasn't a dream.

It was real.

And Sarah wasn't sure how to feel about that other than deeply unsettled.

She staggered through the woods. Trees surrounded her. She felt uneasy, walking past every one of these trees. There could be people standing behind each of them. Hiding. Watching. Waiting to strike.

Or there could be infected. Lurking in the shadows.

Because there was something different about them.

Something *changing* about them.

The infected person. Down the pathway earlier.

The way he'd screamed.

And not a *scream* like an infected, either. But a scream like a person. A child. Like a child who was in danger. Like a child who was terrified. In agony. *That's* what it reminded her of. That's what it was like. Exactly what it was like.

She took a deep breath of the damp, humid air. The woods were dark, but the sky was getting lighter. Almost like a light grey. She could hear birds singing as morning approached. She could smell the warmth—the warmth of the day to follow; that's what it was. And she could taste salt on her dry, cracked lips.

At least she'd had some rest.

Even though it felt like she couldn't afford any rest.

She looked over her shoulder. Back into the darkness. In the direction of the caravan she'd woken up in. Carly's caravan. Carly didn't seem like the friendliest of types. But then that went without saying in this world, didn't it? Sarah was hardly what someone would describe as "friendly" herself, and she knew it. And yet here she was. Searching for her... her *friends*.

It struck her instantly, like waking up from a dream. She thought she wanted to be alone. She thought she wanted to survive for herself. She thought she wanted to go her own way. Because she'd never been one for other people. The only times in her life she'd trusted other people, it'd cost her. And it'd cost her in a big way.

But... it'd almost happened naturally. It'd almost happened by accident.

Keira.

Nisha.

And, yes, even Rufus.

She wanted to find them.

She wanted to make sure they were okay.

Because what Carly told her about the military people—what

she'd told her about *Leonard*... sent an inexplicable shiver down her spine.

She thought about this Leonard character. Carly hadn't told her anything about him other than that he was a military group leader, and he wasn't to be trusted. She didn't elaborate any more than that. Which could mean two things. Either she was just extending her general military scepticism to this man, too, or she was serious about him.

She thought about the men on the road.

The man who'd put the gun to her head.

To Nisha's head.

The way he'd threatened her.

Was he something to do with Leonard's group?

And if he wasn't... did it even matter?

Suddenly, the only thing that mattered was finding Keira. Finding Nisha. Finding wherever they went. Finding them.

But it was Carly she thought about, too.

She looked back again. As cold as Carly seemed, as frosty as she seemed, as stand-offish as she seemed... there was something about her. Something that stood out about her. And Sarah didn't quite realise it at the time. But perhaps there was an element of her, a part to her, that reminded her of herself.

Carly was Sarah if she'd stayed away from other people.

Carly was Sarah if she'd kept on pushing people away.

Carly was Sarah if she hadn't met Keira, David, Nisha, and Rufus.

Carly was Sarah.

But alone.

Like right now.

She looked back ahead into the darkness. She wanted to go back and ask Carly to join her. But Carly didn't seem best pleased about that idea. She was quite happy, isolated in her caravan in the woods.

But Sarah wondered if there was a chance she could come

back here, perhaps. If she couldn't find Keira. If she couldn't find Nisha. If she couldn't find Rufus. Maybe she could come back here. There was something peaceful here in this woods. There was something serene here in this woods.

But for now, she had to focus on what was ahead.

The only thing that was ahead.

Finding Keira.

Finding Nisha.

Finding Rufus.

She knew where she was now. Carly had told her. They weren't far from where Carly first found her. The woods, to the south of that bridlepath. Which meant Sarah wasn't too far from the source of the confrontation in the night.

She wasn't too far off the track from finding the others.

Finding her friends.

She kept on walking through the woods, a small rucksack of supplies over her shoulder that Carly was kind enough to give her. A little bottle of water, almost empty, just enough to "wet her lips," as Carly put it. Half a cereal bar, which was peanut flavoured, something Sarah found sickening, but she wasn't exactly in a position to be fussy. And a blade, too. Well. Barely a blade. More a kitchen knife from a set—and a blunt one at that.

But it would come in handy. She could protect herself with it. If she had to.

She hoped it wouldn't come to that.

She walked further through these woods, the trees growing thicker around her. She didn't know where she was. She was lost. She thought if she walked this way, eventually, she'd link up with the bridlepath again, and she'd be able to trace Keira and the military group's steps right towards wherever they were based.

But she wasn't having much luck.

She wasn't having much luck at all.

She walked another few steps when suddenly she saw something.

At first, she froze. Because she thought it was an infected figure. An infected man standing there. Watching her. Waiting for her.

But it didn't take her long to realise it wasn't an infected man.

It wasn't an infected man at all.

It was a body.

Stripped naked.

Gutted.

Hanging from a tree.

Entrails and innards spilling out of his torn torso.

Flies buzzing around him.

The stench of vomit and shit and off-meat thick in the air.

Sarah's head spun. She felt sick. She felt dizzy. She felt like she might collapse. Like she might pass out.

Especially when she looked to the right.

Especially when she saw another body.

Hanging on a tree right beside this one.

She looked up at them both.

One of them gutted.

One of them, throat slit.

Both of them naked.

And as much as the bodies scared her and their presence filled her with dread, there was something else Sarah noticed.

Something else she noticed, above anything.

The words.

The words smeared across their chests in blood.

WALK AWAY.

She stood there. Shaking. Shivering. She'd taken a wrong turn. She'd taken a wrong turn, and she'd walked right into... into... well, into whatever the fuck this was.

She looked up at the first body. Then, at the second body. Then, the third. The fourth. So many of them. Hanging there. Right in front of her. A boundary. Trying to turn her away.

She just had to walk away from here.

She just had to go back and retrace her steps.

She went to walk away when she heard something.

Something that sent a shiver up her spine.

Something that filled her with fear.

Right behind her.

Right there, in the woods.

A footstep.

Cracking against a branch.

And then another, somewhere off to her left.

She stood there in the woods as fear filled her body, and as these bodies all surrounded her, all stared down at her.

Someone was here.

She wasn't alone.

KEIRA

* * *

It all happened so fast.

The woman. Standing there in the darkness of this bunker. Staring at her with those dead eyes. Blood oozing down her body. And making that blood-curdling groan.

Infected.

Keira's heart raced. Raced so fast it felt like it would burst out of her chest. Like it was going to explode.

The air filled with the smell of damp earthiness.

Her mouth dried up and flooded with the taste of blood.

She stood there. She stared at this woman.

She watched.

She waited.

And then, out of nowhere, the woman launched herself at her.

No sooner had she tried to walk away, tried to step back, tried to run, when she felt something on her arm.

A hand.

A hand. Clamping around her arm. Squeezing into her skin.

Fingernails digging into her flesh.

Somebody had her.

Somebody had her, and they were dragging her into the darkness.

An infected.

The infected she'd heard screaming in the corridor.

They had her.

They had her, and they were going to drag her away, and they were going to kill her, and she wasn't going to be able to help Nisha, she wasn't going to be able to save her, she wasn't…

"Keira!"

A voice. Right beside her. Sending a shiver up her spine.

She looked around.

Around at the source of that voice.

Because it didn't sound like anyone infected.

It sounded like…

A person.

It sounded like…

She looked around, into the darkness, when she saw who it was.

The man. Kevin.

Standing there.

Holding her arm.

Holding his rifle.

"We need to get out," he gasped. "The bunker. We've been compromised. We need to go. Now!"

No sooner did he shout than she heard something down the corridor.

A scream.

No.

A *series* of screams.

Gasps.

Groans.

All racing down the corridor.

All racing down the corridor, through the darkness, towards her.

And the woman.

The woman launching herself out of the room beside her, towards her, and...

Keira swung around.

The woman.

But not just the woman. The *man*, too. The one who'd been lying there, choking, just moments ago.

Now, he was on his feet.

Now, he was racing towards them both, too.

And then...

When Keira saw the child—the little boy in his Pokemon pyjamas—standing there, blood spilling from his throat, glazed eyes staring right up at her, her body went numb.

Kevin lifted his rifle, and he fired blindly into the room.

The bullets splattered against the infected. They fell over against the solid floor. Or maybe they didn't. Keira wasn't sticking around to find out.

She needed to get off this corridor.

They both needed to get off this corridor.

But she saw one thing in the darkness of that room.

In the glow of the gunfire.

The boy.

The infected boy.

Tumbling to the floor.

"Now!" Kevin shouted. Firing back into the darkness. Then, running forward. Holding onto Keira's arm. Her hand digging deep into her skin. Deep into her muscles.

Hard.

She ran down the corridor with Kevin, who fired back into the darkness. The infected screams and cries echoed everywhere. Keira's ears rang with the gunshots. The urgency of the situation grew more and more intense, progressively more and more intense.

But she had to keep going.

She had to keep running.

She had to...

And then suddenly... Nisha.

The door. The door to her left.

Nisha was in there.

Rufus was in there.

She couldn't just leave them.

She couldn't just walk away.

"I can't leave them," Keira said.

Kevin fired another round of bullets back into the dark. "It's too late," he said.

"I can't leave them."

"This place is gone. This place is finished. Everyone... Shit. Everyone's turned. Something's fucking happened. We need to run."

"I'm not leaving her!" Keira shouted.

She looked into Kevin's eyes. Saw him looking back at her, shaking his head, as he held on to the rifle with one hand and onto her arm with the other. He looked devastated. He looked distant. He looked lost. His place. His sanctuary. Everyone was infected. Everyone had turned.

More infected ran down the corridor. Their footsteps slammed against the hard floor. She couldn't see them in the pitch-black darkness. But she could smell them in the air.

The earthiness.

The metallic tang of blood.

Getting closer and closer.

"Now," Kevin said, shaking his head.

"What—"

"Get them. Now. Quick. Then we get the fuck out of here."

He turned around, and he fired at the infected. He was

helping her. He was actually defending this room while she went inside for Nisha, for Rufus.

And... and maybe she could tell him the truth. Maybe she could tell him that Nisha's presence would help. Nisha would help repel the infected. Help deter the infected.

But there wasn't time.

She just had to get in and get them both while she still had the chance.

She opened the door, and her heart sank.

The thought of Nisha and Rufus missing.

Or... dead.

No.

No, she couldn't think like that.

They were going to be okay.

Everything was going to be okay.

And they were going to get out of here.

She slammed the door open, and she saw them both standing there.

Right at the back of the room.

Staring right at her.

"Nisha," she said. "We need to go. Right now."

Nisha stumbled forward. Her nose was bleeding. Heavily.

And she had this look in her eyes.

This look of guilt.

Of sheer guilt.

"Nisha, come on," Keira said, staggering into the room. "We need to get out of here. We need to go. We need to go now."

Nisha stood there.

Kevin's gunfire rang out.

Keira held out her hands.

Nisha stared at her as those infected snarls grew louder.

"Now," Keira said.

And then she ran towards her and grabbed her hands.

Keira turned around. Held Nisha's hand. She ran to the door, to Kevin, Rufus alongside them, towards the darkness.

"It's just down here," Kevin said, pointing up the corridor. "We can get out down..."

A screeching series of echoes right up ahead.

A silence.

A momentary silence.

And then...

More footsteps.

Up ahead.

The way they were supposed to be going.

"Shit," Kevin said.

Keira stood there. Nisha's hand in hers. Rufus barking beside her. Kevin held his gun.

He lifted it.

He pointed it ahead.

He went to fire, and...

And nothing happened.

"Out of ammo," he said. "Out of fucking ammo."

The infected ran closer.

And Keira didn't know what to do.

She didn't know where to go.

She just knew that as reluctant as she'd been on using Nisha as any kind of infected deterrent tool... she was going to need her help getting out of this.

They were all going to need her help getting out of this.

She held Nisha's hand as the infected limped closer when suddenly Kevin pushed her back.

Into the room.

And then he slammed the door shut.

Turned a large, twisting handle.

And then he stood against it, in the total darkness, as the infected smacked at that door behind him.

And it was his face that told her everything.

It was his face that told her more than any words could as the infected banged and scratched and screamed outside.

They were stuck in here.

They were trapped.

And they had no way out.

SARAH

* * *

Sarah stared up at the bodies swinging from the trees and heard the footsteps behind her.

She wasn't alone.

The bodies hung down in the foggy glow of the gradually increasing morning light. The woods were quiet. Deadly quiet, other than her own heavy breathing. Other than her racing heartbeat. Other than the occasional echoing cawing of a crow.

And other than those footsteps.

Inching closer towards her.

The bodies.

The naked, disembowelled bodies.

With words etched across their chests—in blood.

WALK AWAY.

And she intended to. That's absolutely what she intended on doing.

Walking the *hell* away.

But she could hear not one set of footsteps inching towards her, but more than one.

And those sounds.

That made her think she'd already waded just a step too far into enemy territory.

Whoever the enemy was.

She didn't want to find out.

She gulped a heavy lump in her dry throat. A slightly acidic tang coated her lips. Her chest burned and tingled. The familiar taste of dread. Right across her mouth.

She didn't want to turn around. She wanted to run. She just wanted to get the hell away from these hanging bodies. She just wanted to get the hell away from these dangling innards. And she just wanted to get the hell out of these woods and towards Keira, and Nisha, and Rufus—wherever the hell they were.

But she turned around.

Slowly.

She held her breath.

And...

From where she'd heard the footsteps, something struck her. Not literally. Figuratively. Thankfully.

And the thing that struck her more than anything?

There was no one in sight.

She stood there. Heart racing. She looked around at the trees, all standing so tall, close, and compressed. She saw the grey sky above. She heard that crow cawing overhead. And the more she stood there, the more she squinted, the more she wondered if maybe she'd imagined those footsteps. Maybe she'd just imagined them, and they were all a part of her mind—all a figment of her imagination. A thoroughly creeped-out imagination.

And then she heard another crack of a branch, and somewhere to her right, she saw movement.

It was only slight. It was just in the corner of her eyes.

But it was there.

It was right there. And there was nothing she could do to ignore it.

There was no doubt about it.

It was movement.

It wasn't in her imagination.

Someone was there.

She turned around and saw a figure darting behind a tree.

Disappearing behind a tree.

Her skin turned cold. Her heart raced faster. She gripped hold of the knife Carly handed her. Gripped it with her shaking hand. And the nerves. Maybe it was the nerves, but that dread. It was making her back hurt even more. It was making her legs shake. It was making that throbbing, burning agony grow in intensity.

She stood there. Back to the bodies. She could see the woods opening up in front of her. So many places to run.

But at the same time... nowhere to hide.

Because someone was in here with her.

Someone was watching her.

Someone was watching her closely.

Very closely.

She wanted to run, but her legs were like jelly.

She wanted to sprint away but didn't even have the energy or strength to do so.

She wanted to get away.

But she was stuck here.

She was trapped here.

Right on the spot.

She stood there. Heart racing. Sweat pouring down her face.

She needed to run.

She needed to get away.

And then she heard something right behind her.

Something that filled her with fear.

Barking.

A deep, loud barking.

She ran.

Ran as fast as she could.

Tree branches slapped and scratched her face.

Branches split underfoot, and her balance wobbled. She stumbled from side to side. The pain shooting up her legs. Twisting its way up and into her spine. You can do this, Sarah. You're going to be okay. You can get away. You can do this.

She ran further as the barking grew even louder behind her and even closer. She saw figures in her periphery. And she could *hear* them, too. Unless... unless it was all in her head, all in her imagination.

No.

She could hear them.

Whispering amongst themselves.

And the barking.

She had to get out of these woods.

She had to get away.

But there was nowhere to run.

She looked over her shoulder. Which she knew was a mistake right away. An instinctive fucking mistake, but a mistake all the same.

And when she looked back... she saw it.

A dog.

No.

A fucking *monster* of a dog. Bully XL type. Although this looked like a Bully XXXL if there were such a thing.

Drool dangling from the sides of its gaping mouth.

Blood-soaked white teeth, so long, so sharp.

Chasing her.

Closing in on her with its muscular body.

Barking at her.

Snarling at her.

Shit. Maybe she was wrong about dogs. Maybe she really, really didn't like dogs after all.

And behind the dog... she saw figures. Two people. Men in tracksuits, sprinting after her—or after their dog, it was hard to tell. But they were holding machetes. Long machetes. And they had their hoods up. Yeah. They didn't look like the kind of men who would invite her around for dinner.

She turned back around. Almost slammed into a tree. Almost fell over. She kept on running. Kept on going. She didn't know what to do. Where to go. What to think.

She could only keep running through those trees.

Keep dodging those trees.

As the dog barks got closer.

As the footsteps of the pursuers got closer.

As they all closed in on her, and...

Suddenly, a sharp sensation across her right ankle.

An involuntary, instinctive cry emitted from her lungs.

She tumbled over.

Looked around.

And as she lay there, going dizzy, head spinning, everything fuzzing around her... she saw that monster dog.

Clamped down on her ankle.

Teeth piercing into her jeans.

Tearing into her skin.

And the men with machetes inching closer.

"Good lad," one of them said, a balaclava wrapped around his face as he wrestled back his monstrous beast of a dog. "You got her, boy. Good lad..."

CARLY

* * *

Carly watched the Sarah chick walk away and had to admit she felt kind of empty about it.

Not *sad*. Just... yeah. Empty.

It was morning again. The sun would be rising soon. She always got up for sunrise. Nothing spiritual or anything like that. Didn't really care for any of that bullshit. But she figured soon, the nights would be drawing in. Soon, darkness would accompany her for the bulk of the day.

And the thought of spending months in total darkness with nothing but the biters for company?

Yeah. That shit depressed Carly.

The wind whistled through the trees. The birds sang from above, their morning call gradually getting louder. It sounded pretty. She'd always loved birds. When she was younger, other kids seemed more interested in other animals. She remembered a project once at primary school where everyone had to draw a picture of their favourite animal.

Kids drew lions. Kids drew sharks. Kids drew their pet dogs. And some even drew dinosaurs.

Carly?

She drew a fucking robin that used to visit her garden back at the flat.

Well. Not *her* garden. She wasn't lucky enough to have a garden of her own. But she liked to pretend it *was* her garden. Because the others' kids had gardens. The other kids drew pictures of their gardens. They drew pictures of their holidays. They drew so many nice damned fucking pictures.

So, yeah. Carly drew the birds that weren't actually her birds in a garden that wasn't actually her garden.

When life hands you lemons, right?

Was that even the fucking saying?

She listened to the birds right now, and she felt... kind of relaxed. In a sort of spiritual way that she hadn't really been too kind to just a few moments earlier. We're all fucking hypocrites at heart, right? Whether we're the hypocrite or we're *fucking* the hypocrite, the law of odds says there's some hypocrisy in there.

Okay. That one might stay funnier in her head.

Usually, Carly slept like a log. She slept great. Woke up early. Watched the sunrise. Appreciated the light, from the start to the very end.

But these last few days had been different.

Because of the dreams.

She kept dreaming of a girl.

A girl she'd never met. She was... chained up somewhere. Chained up in some room. Some small, damp room. Terrified. Lost. Alone.

And it seemed like this kid was *speaking* to her in some way. Like she had a voice, but her lips weren't moving, and... Yeah. Bat shit crazy. Carly wasn't a fucking idiot. She knew how it sounded.

But somehow, it didn't feel like a dream to her.

Somehow, it felt... real to her.

So the last few nights had been disturbed by these vivid dreams. Dreams of this kid. Begging her to join her. Begging her to help her. She kept on saying where she was. The North Lancs barracks. Somewhere her dad had taken her.

Only... Carly wasn't going anywhere near the North Lancs barracks.

The less said about the North Lancs barracks—the less said about Leonard—the better.

A shiver crept down her spine at the mere thought of Leonard.

Don't go there.

But this morning was different. She got caught out in the night by a group of infected. Biggest group she'd ever seen. All wading their way along in this massive group. So many people. No wonder the streets had been quiet for a couple of days. Was that what the infected did now? Congregate? She couldn't decide whether that was a good or a bad thing. Probably depended on context. Good if you were behind them. Bad if you were right in front of the fuckers.

This morning she'd been walking back from the middle of fucking nowhere when she ran into a woman. Dangling from a tree. The poor fucker was stupid enough to get herself stuck up a tree.

And for that alone, she kind of wanted to leave her to die.

But she hadn't.

Something had stopped Carly from leaving her. Call it a conscience. Call it whatever. Something had stopped her. She'd helped her. Used valuable bullets from the rifle she'd taken from one of Leonard's dead cunts and helped clear a path for her.

Then she'd put her over her shoulder and taken her back to her caravan.

And now...

Now, that woman—Sarah—she was walking away.

Carly took a deep breath. Sighed. She didn't know why she felt so empty about it. She wasn't one for other people. She had her reasons. People didn't tend to like her. And when they *did* tend to like her, people tended to take advantage of her because she was stupid enough to let her walls drop enough for them to take the piss.

But Sarah. Having someone else here, even if just for a little while. Looking after someone while they were suffering. She had to admit, that felt kind of nice.

No.

No, don't think like that.

Think about all the other reasons you have not to trust people.

Not to let them in.

'Cause God knows you have more than enough fucking reasons.

She took a deep breath.

Swallowed a lump in her throat.

Looked into the trees.

Wherever this Sarah woman was… she hoped she was okay.

She looked down at her arm.

Looked at the patch of blood covering her forearm.

Pulled her sleeve down just a little.

She didn't need to think about that. Not right now.

She didn't need to think about *anything* right now.

The reason she was out here. On her own.

The reason she had to be away from other people.

She just had to hope Sarah was different.

She stared out at the rising light outside, and she took a deep breath of the morning air, and she thought about the girl from her dreams…

KEIRA

* * *

Keira stood in the middle of the dark makeshift bedroom in the depths of the bunker.

A bunker that seemed like salvation such a short time ago.

A bunker that now felt like a tomb.

The fists of the infected slammed against the metal door. Their cries grew louder and more desperate. So many of them. So, so many of them, trapped down here with them.

And she knew there was no way out.

It was pitch black in here. The candles had gone out. She had no idea what time of day it was. Whether it was a bright summer day outside, beyond these walls, or the dead of night. She saw Kevin, hands on his knees, right beside the door, shaking his head. Still clinging on to that rifle, even though it was out of ammo. Almost as if the mere fact of him holding the rifle might deter some of the infected from attacking.

She saw Nisha right beside her. Still awake. Still conscious. Still fucking *alive*. Which was a blessing. An absolute blessing that she hadn't even had the time to process. That she hadn't even had the time to wrap her head around. To contemplate.

She was here. Rufus was here.

They were all here, in this room.

But they were trapped.

The infected continued to cry behind the solid metal bunker door. They continued to bang. And now and then, Keira heard a different kind of cry. Like someone was being attacked. Like someone was begging. Begging for their lives. Infected? Or... or just an infected person *imitating* a pained, suffering person? Because that was a possibility, too. It was a horrible new possibility she was having to get to grips with. That they were all having to get to grips with.

And it made everything even more difficult to comprehend.

The room smelled of sweat. And of blood. This room. It was going to become their tomb. The infected weren't going to walk away. They weren't going to give up. They had an easy meal waiting here for them behind that door. They just had to wait until they figured out how to open the can, so to speak.

She chuckled a bit at that. At her own thought. Sometimes, in the darkest of moments, it was humour that sparked up above any other emotion. Comedy and horror, they weren't too dissimilar. They weren't too far apart, were they?

You had to laugh in the dark moments. You just had to laugh at the absurdity of it all. The sheer fuckery of it all. Because what were the chances? What were the chances that Keira just happened to be alive at the time of a fucking—let's call it what it is—zombie outbreak? Okay. It might not exactly be dead people breaking out of their coffins and dragging themselves out of the earth. But it was as much of a zombie outbreak as the one in 28 Days Later was—and as much as people debated the credentials of that movie as a pure "zombie" movie... fuck. What was she even thinking? Why the hell was she thinking about zombie movies right now? She was living in one.

And it was about to come to a very grisly end.

She took Nisha's hand. Squeezed it just a bit. Her fingers felt cold. Shaky. Almost as if she knew something bad was happening beyond those doors. Even though she couldn't hear, she wasn't an idiot. She could see very damned well that something was happening.

She thought about the note. The one she'd written.

The words.

Those words scribbled across it.

I did something bad.

What did that mean?

What did it have to do with the sudden onslaught of infected surging through this bunker?

Another bang slammed against the door. Another series of infected groans echoed into the room. What did they do? Because if there were no way out… maybe they would have to see whether Nisha could use her abilities. That wasn't something Keira wanted to do. It wasn't something she wanted to turn to. Not particularly. Nisha had suffered enough. She'd been through enough. She didn't want to keep on using her as a deterrent. Especially when she'd just barely survived whatever happened to her yesterday…

"What do we do?" Keira asked.

Kevin rubbed his fingers across his head. "There's not a lot we *can* do."

Keira swallowed a lump in her throat. She tightened her grip around Nisha's hand.

"This infection. Everyone… everyone was clear. There was nobody infected in here."

Nisha's words replayed in Keira's mind.

I've done something bad.

Did she tell him the truth? No. She couldn't tell him about Nisha. Not now. Not while he was in this state. Not while he was in this frame of mind. He'd just witnessed the collapse of his home. He'd just witnessed so many people—so many *friends*—succumb to the infection. Military friends. Civilians they'd dragged off the street and saved. He'd just shot them all. One by one. Now wasn't the time for making any admissions about Nisha.

And now they were stuck in here.

Now, they were trapped.

"I don't understand how this can happen," Kevin said.

"We don't know how the infection works—"

"Nobody was bitten," he said. Looking up at Keira. Almost snapping at her, now. "Nobody was..."

And then his eyes settled. For just a second, for just a moment, the look on his face shifted.

He looked at Keira, and how he looked at her... it was as if he was piecing something together.

Like he was connecting the dots in his head.

"We never checked you properly."

"Kevin," Keira said.

Kevin stood up. "If you've nothing to hide, you'll show me. Okay? Prove it to me. Both of you. Prove to me you aren't infected."

Keira's heart raced. Behind Kevin, behind that door, she heard the infected slamming at the door, trying to break inside.

"Show me!" he shouted.

And she got it. She really got it. This man's people had just fallen. His home was compromised. He was trying to make sense of it.

And...

And maybe he was right.

Maybe it was something to do with Nisha.

I've done something bad.

But how?

How?

"I trusted you," Kevin said. His voice faltering. Like he was making his mind up before he even knew the truth. "I was stupid. I was blinded by... Fuck. What have I done? What have I done?"

Keira's heart raced. She didn't know what to say.

"I let you in, and I trusted you and..." He took a deep breath. Inhaled deeply. "Show me. Prove to me this wasn't you. Please."

Keira looked at Nisha.

She tightened her grip around her hand.

She couldn't tell him.

She couldn't risk Nisha.

But what other choice did she have?

"Kevin," she said. "You need to know it's not what it looks like..."

But he wasn't listening.

She could tell he wasn't listening.

Because he was looking at something.

Something on the floor, right in front of him.

Keira looked down at where he was looking, and she saw it.

She saw what he was looking at.

Exactly what he was looking at.

Her stomach sank.

He looked down at it. Picked it up. Read it. Studied it.

And then he looked across at Keira.

Then, at Nisha.

"What..." he started.

Because he was holding the note.

The note that Nisha had written.

I've done something bad.

He stood there. Hand shaking. Note quivering between his fingers.

"Kevin—"

"No," Kevin said, shaking his head. Crumpling the piece of paper up.

"It's not what it looks like—"

"Prove it wasn't you," he said.

Keira shook her head.

"Prove it wasn't you, Keira. Or the girl. The..."

And then his eyes widened. As if the realisation was flashing across his face. The realisation. Nisha's unconsciousness. Her sickness. All coming together in his mind.

"How could I be so stupid," he said.

And she knew she had to talk now.

She knew there was no hiding.

Not anymore.

"Kevin, she was bitten, but she hasn't turned."

But Kevin wasn't listening.

He was just shaking his head.

Shaking his head as the infected slammed at the door behind him.

"She's different," Keira said. "Even before she was bitten, she could repel them. She could hold back the infected. She..."

But Kevin wasn't listening.

He was just shaking his head.

Crying.

"I trusted you," he said. "I let you in. On faith. And you killed them. You killed my people."

Keira shook her head. She didn't understand this any better than he did.

She didn't know what'd happened.

She didn't know what was going on.

She just knew that something *had* happened.

And somehow, as much as she tried to hide from it, as much as she tried to deny it, Nisha *was* involved.

And no matter what she said or how much she tried to bargain... Kevin wasn't going to come around to her way of thinking.

He wasn't going to see what she was saying.

"You killed my people," Kevin said. "And it's on me. It's my fault. It's..."

And then she saw something.
A glint of something.
Flickering in his right hand.
A knife.
A blade.
Shaking between his fingers.
She took a step back.
"Kevin," she said. Holding up a hand. "Nisha can help us out of here."
But Kevin wasn't hearing a thing. He was caught deep in the thick fog of suffering.
He was just walking towards her.
Gripping that shaking knife.
"She's different. She can stop them. She can help us."
But Kevin really wasn't listening.
He just kept on walking towards her.
One step after another.
Echoing towards her.
That knife in his hand.
Tears streaming down his face.
Sobbing.
"I trusted you," he said. "And you did this. You did *this*."
She watched him take another step towards her.
Towards Nisha.
Towards Rufus, who growled, who barked, stepping back, hackles raised.
She stood there as the infected snarls echoed through the corridor.
She stood there as Kevin took another step closer, holding that knife, raising that knife.
And she could only stand there as he hurled towards Nisha and swung that knife right at her.

SARAH

* * *

Sarah felt the pain spreading all the way up her right leg, and she knew she was well and truly screwed.

It was pitch black. Not outside. Of that much, she was rather certain. But because of the blindfold that had been wrapped around her eyes the moment that crew reached her position. Her right ankle was agony. Total agony. The dog. The ugly XL Bully bastard. It'd caught up with her. Ripped right into her skin, deep into the muscle.

And all she could think of, as that splitting bite pain spread deeper into her leg?

How sorry she felt for everyone who had been bitten by the infected.

Because those bites. They were agony. Total agony.

So agonising that she hadn't really been able to think of anything else while they bound her wrists, while they blindfolded her, and while they dragged her away towards God knows where.

And the pain was still bad. Almost insufferable, in fact.

Certainly took the focus away from her aching back, that was for sure.

But even though the pain was bad, she could focus a little on her predicament now, at least.

And it wasn't a very appealing focus, to say the least.

So she was in the dark. And her leg was on fire. She'd been taken somewhere. She didn't know where. Now, she was in some sort of room on her own. She could hear muffled talking. Muffled chatter outside somewhere. The blindfold around her head was so tight it felt like the top of her skull might just burst off.

She was gagged, too. The gag tasted bad. So bad. Like pure shit. Made her want to heave. But she knew heaving was a bad idea, logically, because if she threw up, she'd probably end up choking on her own vomit or something awful like that.

Even in the most awful of circumstances, she had to remain logical.

She tried to move her hands. But they were bound behind her back. The ties dug deep into her wrists. So deep that she could feel her fingers tingling, turning cold. Her ankles were tied together in front of her, too. She was sitting down, knees in front of her. She didn't know where she was. But after seeing those bodies dangling from the trees a little while back, in the middle of the woods, with the *WALK AWAY* etched across their chests... she could only imagine that's where she'd ended up.

And it went without saying that the company of those lunatics was quite literally the last place she wanted to end up.

But what could she do about it?

She was bound at the ankles.

She was bound at the wrists.

She was blindfolded, and she was gagged.

Whoever had captured her wanted to keep her here.

They didn't want her going anywhere.

She sat there. She could hear something trickling. Dripping against the solid metal floor. Was it her bleeding ankle? Shit. It needed attention. They'd bandaged it up a little bit, but as far as she could tell, they hadn't cleaned the wound or stitched it or anything like that.

And that made her wonder what the intentions of these people were.

It made her wonder what they wanted.

Exactly what they wanted.

She tried to yank her wrists apart.

She tried to yank her ankles apart.

She tried to shuffle free of the blindfold and the gag.

But she couldn't.

She just couldn't.

She went to pull her wrists apart again when suddenly, she heard something.

Approaching her.

Footsteps.

She froze. Her heart pounded. Her chest tightened.

Because whoever was approaching her they weren't a good person. That much was obvious.

Whoever was approaching her... they were bad.

Really bad.

The footsteps echoed closer towards her.

Inched closer and closer.

And was that... *panting* she could hear?

A panting dog.

The XL Bully.

The one that'd bitten her.

Shit.

She sat there, frozen. Stared up into the darkness. The footsteps had stopped. But the panting. The rattling chain. Both of those were still loud. Both of those were close.

And she swore she could smell that dog's ghastly breath, too.

Damn. Bad breath. A bite wound. What if the wound got infected? And not infected in a "zombie" kind of way. Just *infected*.

A good old-fashioned infection. The glory days of septic shock seemed a long way away.

She held her breath and waited when suddenly, light filled her eyes.

She was in some kind of garage. It wasn't airtight. She could see light peeking through various holes in the brick. And the join that connected the metal roof with the structure. It was dirty in here. Various old tools lay around—garden tools, by the looks of things. An old freezer and a dryer. A bicycle beside her, tires punctured.

Yes. This was someone's garage area.

A man stood over her.

He was much like the men who'd kidnapped her. Who'd taken her.

He was tall. Skinny. Wore all black. Had a hood up, right over his head.

And he wore a balaclava, too. Covering his mouth.

A black balaclava.

With white dots peppered over it.

He held on to a chain lead with this huge XL Bully on the end of it. A drooling, growling, gasping mess of ugly, inbred meat. Staring at Sarah with these angry, possessed eyes. Trying to pull towards her. Trying to get closer to her. The same dog as the one who attacked her? She didn't think so. That one was more of a brown colour. This one looked more on the black side. Great. So there was more than one of these monsters here? Perfect. Just what she wanted.

The man stood over her. Stared down at her. Holding her blindfold in the same hand that was holding a baseball bat.

A baseball bat covered in nails.

Bloody nails.

He stared at her with these sinister eyes. Impossible to see the humanity to him because of the balaclava.

And Sarah had no idea how long he stood there. How long he

stared down at her. How long this suffocating silence stretched on.

But eventually... he spoke.

"You were on our land," he said.

Sarah narrowed her eyes. She was still gagged, so she couldn't say a word.

"We warned you. With the signs. We warn people to stay away. If they don't, that's their own fuckin' fault."

Warned her? To stay off his land? With the WALK AWAY marks etched into people's chests? Fucking prick. She'd only seen the bodies dangling there a few seconds before these creeps were onto them. So, was that what this was? Some bizarre justification for their actions—whatever their actions were? You were on our land, so whatever happens next is fair game? Was that it?

And besides. Who was this man to talk about "their land" at all? It was a matter of weeks since the outbreak began. Was this what society had descended to already? Power crazy lunatics? Or was there more to this?

She would love to ask.

But the gag was making that rather difficult.

"I won't lie," the man said, loosening the chain lead a little, letting the XL Bully inch closer. The dog snapped its jaws. Barked. More drool oozed down from its enormous teeth. "Things aren't looking good for you."

And then he loosened the lead some more.

"But there is a way out."

A way out. Perfect. Of course, there was a way out.

"Your people. The place you came from. You can lead us there. We can do a deal. You can let us take what you have."

Wait, what? Her people? The place she came from? She didn't come from anywhere. She didn't have *people* in the way he seemed to be implying.

"You lead us there, and we let you live. We let you have some of the best shit we've got. We'll look after you. For having our backs. We'll have yours."

He pulled the dog back just a little.

"But if you don't..."

The dog inched closer again.

"If you ain't got nowt to offer us... or if you won't cooperate..."

He lifted the baseball bat.

A little blood dripped from the end of one of the nails.

"Then we'll have to find a new use for you, won't we?"

He looked down at her.

Looked down at her with those sinister eyes.

Underneath his balaclava, Sarah swore she saw the man smile.

NISHA

* * *

Nisha didn't know what the man in the army clothes was talking about or why he looked so mad.

But she could guess right away that it had something to do with her, just from how he looked at her.

He was looking at her like her teachers looked at her when she was in trouble. Which was quite a lot. She didn't mean to be naughty. Dad always told her not to be naughty. That the world was "already against her," whatever that meant, she guessed it was something to do with her deafness.

But it was just hard. It was hard being deaf. It was hard trying to learn stupid things like maths and science when she couldn't hear anything and when she wasn't gonna need any of it anyway.

But right now, she kind of wished she was back in maths class again.

The man looked at her. He was shouting something. And he was walking closer towards her with a knife. Keira was shouting back at him, too. Shaking her head. Holding Nisha's hand. Tight.

And Nisha didn't know where she was. These people. She

didn't know what they wanted. But it looked like Keira wasn't scared of them at first, and now she was.

And Rufus. He didn't look happy either. He was standing there. Growling. His mouth was moving. Like he was barking.

And the man walking towards her was bad.

And then there were the dreams.

Or were they memories?

Maybe that would be a better thing to call them.

Because that's what they were, right?

She remembered walking. Walking in those dreams.

Walking down the dark corridor.

She remembered that voice in her head.

Telling her to do it.

Telling her not to fight it.

Telling her she was powerful, and she needed to let them all see what she could do.

And then...

She remembered entering the man's body.

She remembered filling his veins with *herself*.

And then it wasn't just this one man.

It was *other* people, too.

Rushing into their heads.

Seeing them all at once, like she was watching loads of different television screens.

And all the time, she could see this... REDNESS.

She could *feel* this voice inside her.

Telling her how powerful she was.

Telling her how strong she was.

She let it flood between them, between all of them, this anger, this rage, even though she knew it was bad, even though she knew it was wrong, she jumped between each of them and...

And then she saw Keira.

She saw Keira, and she heard the whisper.

Heard it.

Understood it.

Take her too, dear.

Show her the better side.

She saw Keira, and she wanted to fight, she wanted to stop, she wanted to hold back, when...

The girl.

The girl from her dreams.

Chained up.

Staring at her.

Staring right into her eyes.

She wasn't saying anything anymore. Or maybe she was, and Nisha just couldn't hear her.

But *seeing* her.

Just seeing her was enough to break the spell.

No don't don't fight don't resist don't, dear, don't—

And then she was awake again.

She shot up. Sat right up. She could taste blood. She could taste sweat. And she felt really tired and sick. Really, really tired and sick.

And even though it felt like she'd been asleep for a long time... she wondered if it was all in her head. Everything that'd happened since she collapsed with Sarah. Now, she was with Keira. She was with Keira and Rufus, and there was this man across from her.

But deep down, she knew something was wrong. She could see it on his face. And from the way he was walking towards her.

With that knife.

And she could see the door behind him moving a bit, too.

Shaking.

Rattling.

She could smell it.

She could *feel* it.

They were getting closer.

They were getting closer, and they were stronger than before. They felt like they were getting stronger now. Like the more she held them back, the more she stopped them, they were getting stronger every time.

Unless she was just getting... weaker.

The man stopped. Right in front of her. Right in front of Keira. Right in front of Rufus.

And Keira tightened her grip around Nisha's hand as the man looked down at her.

He stood there.

Knife in hand.

Wide eyes peering down at her.

And she didn't know what was happening until suddenly, he fell because Keira hit him with something, something that smashed all over his face.

And then the next minute, the man lifted the knife and swung it back at Keira and...

The door.

The door.

Shaking.

Rattling.

The smell.

So close.

And the feeling.

That feeling deep inside her body.

The feeling she couldn't explain.

The feeling she couldn't describe.

Just that she knew what she had to do.

She looked down at Keira. At the man. Pinning her down. Holding her to the floor.

She looked at Rufus.

And there was something different about Rufus.

Something different about the way he was looking at her.

He was growling.

At her.

She turned around from Rufus, and she walked over to the door.

Because that's what the feeling told her to do.

The feeling that felt like: *yes dear walk walk to the door let them in let us in we can be one we can be together we can all be together we can all be mother.*

She grabbed the handle with her shaking hand.

She held her breath.

She looked around at Keira.

At the man.

The knife raised over her.

Yes now yes let us in let us in let us...

She gulped.

She turned back around.

And then she did the only thing that felt right, right now.

Nisha opened the door to the bad people.

SARAH

* * *

Sarah sat in the garage, completely alone in the darkness.
And even though she wasn't a defeatist kind of person, she couldn't shake the feeling that her luck in this world was about to come crashing to a very unsavoury end.

The garage she was trapped in was pitch-black but for a few cracks of light around the edges of the corrugated steel roof. She could hear rain trickling down the gaps in it, echoing against the solid concrete floor. The smell of metal hung around the air. Rusty metal. The old tools in this garage? Or the blood seeping from her ankle? That damned XL Bully. The little—or big—shit had done a real number on her.

She sat there. Mouth dry. Lips chapped. She felt sick. Sick with nerves. And sick with the gradual blood loss, too, no doubt. Because make no mistake about it. She was losing a lot of blood. That monster of a dog, it'd bitten deep. Really deep.

She wasn't blindfolded anymore. Or gagged. She didn't want to look down at her leg again. She didn't want to acknowledge the blood loss. She didn't want to acknowledge the puncture wounds, pumping blood out. But she kept on looking. Perhaps with morbid fascination. Perhaps just to remind herself that no matter what she did here, there was no way out. There was no getting away. She was screwed. Well and truly screwed.

She closed her burning eyes and felt sleepy right away. Shit. She opened her eyes, then. She couldn't let herself drift off. Drifting off was accepting her fate. Drifting off was accepting death. She couldn't accept death. She couldn't accept her fate. She wasn't ready to accept her fate. Not just yet.

She sat there on this hard, cold floor. A few rat droppings peppered around her. Her vision blurring, colours flickering in her eyes. Her head getting a little dizzy, a little woozy. Drifting a little. Her heart racing fast, which was probably a terrible fucking thing because it would be pumping the blood to her leaking leg even more.

She sat there, and she felt defeated. She sat there, and she felt weak.

She sat there, and she thought of Dean.

The cupboard. The cupboard he used to make her go in. The cupboard he used to lock her in when she hadn't been "behaving." The cupboard he locked her in to punish her. Because she needed punishing. So many times, she needed punishing, even though the bulk of the time, she wasn't even sure what she was supposed to have done wrong.

And that said it all about his treatment of her, really.

He'd ground her down to the point that she didn't even doubt that she'd done something wrong. She figured she was unusual. So she just hadn't realised exactly what she'd done. She didn't know. Not for sure.

But she just accepted that she must've done something wrong.

Because Dean knew best.

Dean always knew best.

She tensed her fists, then. She opened her eyes. She took in a deep, shaky breath of the clammy, damp, soily air.

She sat there in the darkness, her heart racing.

And she knew, as she sat there, that she couldn't just accept her fate.

She couldn't just let these people get the better of her.

The man. The man in the balaclava holding the dog.

The way he'd crouched opposite her.

The words he'd said to her.

"You lead us there, and we let you live. But if you don't... we'll have to find a new use for you, won't we?"

The demand. The demand to take him back to her people or darker horrors would await.

Only she didn't *have* people to the extent he was suggesting. To the extent he was hoping.

Right now, it was just her.

She had no idea where Keira and Nisha had been taken to. Okay, a rough idea, perhaps.

But even if she had a specific idea, there's no way she'd give up their location.

She remembered those words.

"We'll have to find a new use for you, won't we?"

And that slight smile to his mouth when he'd said those words.

She felt the pain in her ankle, shook her head, and took another deep breath.

Then she yanked her wrists apart.

Hard.

The ties. The ties didn't move. Not at all. And moving the ones around her ankles, trying to separate those just made her legs feel like they were going to split open. Like they were going to burst.

But she tried anyway.

She yanked her wrists apart.

She yanked her ankles apart.

She tried, and she tried, as splitting pain stung her legs, stung her wrists.

And as her heart raced harder, and she grew dizzier.

She kept on going. Kept on trying to separate them. She was stronger than these ties. They weren't much. They'd underestimated her by tying her up in these.

She could break them.

She could get out of them.

She could...

She tried, and tried, and tried.

But no matter how much she tried, how hard she tried, there was no luck.

No luck whatsoever.

She wasn't getting out of these ties.

She was trapped.

She went to drag her ankles apart one final time—more in a moment of futile hope than anything—when something remarkable happened.

Something entirely unexpected.

Her ankles.

They split free of the ties.

She looked down at her ankles. Saw the blood seeping through the shitty makeshift bandage loosely tied around her leg.

The ties hung on either side of her legs.

But her legs.

They were free.

She sat there for a few seconds. Stared at them. Heart racing. Unprepared. Unprepared for this possibility. For this eventuality. Because this. This wasn't supposed to happen. This wasn't supposed to be how it was. She'd only been trying to break free in some sort of faint hope. But this...

She had to get out of here.

She had to get to her feet.

She had to move.

She stood up. Her back ached. And, fuck, her leg. Her leg was even worse than she thought. Blood seeping out the second she put any pressure on it. Her head growing dizzier, spinning.

She gritted her teeth. Tasted blood as she chewed her cheeks on the sides of her tongue.

She had to keep going.

She had to stay strong.

She staggered across the garage floor. Towards that door. It'd be locked. It wouldn't be open. There was no getting out of here. There was no way out of here.

But she had to keep walking.

She had to try.

She reached the door.

Grabbed the handle.

Went to turn it, expecting it to be locked, expecting the handle not to turn, when something similarly amazing happened.

The handle.

It lowered.

Her heart pounded harder. Wait. It was... it was *unlocked?*

And if it was unlocked, she could get out of here. She could get away. It might not be easy. It might not be straightforward. And she still had to be careful. She still had to watch out. Because there could be people out there. They could see her escaping. Chase her.

And the state of her leg right now and the pain crippling her body, she didn't fancy her chances being chased right now.

She kept that handle lowered.

Took a deep breath.

Swallowed a lump in her throat.

And then she pushed the door open.

When the door swung open, she smelled the clammy air seeping in. She saw light filling this dismal garage. She felt a momentary sense of relief seeping right into her body and through her bones.

But that didn't last long.

It didn't last long at all.

Because a man was standing there.

A man wearing a balaclava.

Looking right at her with smiling eyes.

The man who'd threatened her.

Standing right there.

Hood up.

Staring at her.

"Going somewhere?" he said.

She tried to dart around him.

She tried to race past him.

She tried to force herself beyond him.

But then he just grabbed her arms.

Held her in place.

And then, with a surprising, sudden strength, he booted her on the bite on her right ankle.

Hard.

CARLY

* * *

Carly held on to the rifle, walked through the woods, and wondered what in the name of Hell she was even thinking by attempting what she was trying.

It was morning. Light. A little rainy. Grim. Stuffy. Muggy. Hated mornings like this. She felt tired. She'd been up a bit already in the caravan. Up with sunrise, as already established. Staring off into the distance as she watched the sunrise.

Usually, she took those moments as an opportunity for quiet time. A chance for letting her thoughts go, for emptying her mind. For being one with nature.

But this morning, she hadn't found any time to relax.

This morning, she couldn't stop thinking about something in particular.

Or some*one* in particular.

The woman.

Sarah.

She walked past the thickening mass of trees. Her heart pounded. What was she doing? What in the name of God was she doing? She should've stayed in the caravan. She should've stayed in the caravan, and she should be keeping herself safe. Not going off in pursuit of some woman she'd only known for a few frigging hours in the grand scheme of things. Less when you consider the amount of time that Sarah chick was actually *conscious*.

But... there was something about her. She had to admit it. There was something about Sarah that made Carly step out of her caravan and march through the damned woods in the middle of the morning like a fucking idiot. Like a fucking lunatic.

She didn't know what it was.

But perhaps there was something in Sarah that reminded her of herself.

Perhaps something in Sarah made her realise there was more to life than just... loneliness.

She heard the birds singing in the trees. Some of them flew off when she passed by, crunching through the fallen branches on the ground. The air was thick with the smell of damp. It was the other smell she had to be more conscious of. The smell of rain on a hot day.

The unmistakable smell of the biters.

She gulped. She was hungry. But she didn't really have much of an appetite. If that even made any sense at all. She felt like if she ate, she might throw up. It wouldn't be the first time. It reminded her of the past. It reminded her of Munich. It reminded her of... things she'd rather forget.

But here she was. Walking. Walking through the woods. The cool drizzle coating her, soaking her to the skin. And as she walked, the further she got, the more convinced she grew that this was a terrible idea. That she needed to go back. She needed to go back to the caravan. She needed to go back to her new home. To the only real home she'd had since...

No.

No, don't go there either.

Don't think about it.

Don't think about the darkness.

Don't think about the screams.

Don't think about the horrible meals and the smell of burned sugar clinging to skin and...

Just think about now.

She walked further through the woods, admittedly with no real idea *why* she was on this journey other than a vague sense that somehow, Sarah was worth saving, when she saw something dangling from up ahead.

From the trees.

Bodies.

Disembowelled bodies.

Swinging from the branches.

WALK AWAY etched across their chests.

In blood.

She looked up at them, and her skin went cold. Shit. Sarah had gone walking this way. There were prints on the ground, in the mud. She'd gone walking right this way, towards these bodies, the sickly sweet smell, that grey skin, that drained blood, and those vacant eyes.

She stopped, then. Heart pounding. She had to turn back. She couldn't keep walking. She had to turn back, and she had to walk away. Sure, Sarah seemed like a good person. But she wasn't her problem anymore. These people, whoever they are, they weren't good people. They weren't people she wanted to risk messing with.

But...

She looked through the trees. She looked ahead. Somewhere in the distance, she could hear muffled voices. She could smell a hint of smoke in the air. And she could taste the burning, too. Like barbecued meat.

She gripped her rifle tight. She only had a few bullets. And the rifle wasn't exactly the most reliable.

And she wondered whether she wanted to do this.

Whether she wanted to risk this.

Because there was no guarantee Sarah had even gone this way.

There was no guarantee she was even heading in the right direction.

But what if she was?

She looked down the slope. Towards the burning. Towards the muffled laughter.

She looked over her shoulder. Back towards her caravan. Back towards her silent sanctuary. Back towards her home.

And then she felt this fear. This fear in the pit of her stomach.

This fear clawing its way through her body.

She didn't want to risk it.

She didn't want to open herself up to *them* again.

But something told her that was what she needed to do.

Exactly what she needed to do.

She took a deep breath.

Closed her eyes.

And just like that, with a click of a finger... she saw them.

She saw the biters.

She saw them surrounding her.

And she saw through their eyes.

The second she saw through their eyes, she felt them being drawn to her.

Drawn to her like a magnet.

Like she was a beacon, springing online and suddenly drawing them all to her.

And then she heard the voice.

You can't play with us for too long.

Your luck will run out.

Mother will consume you.

She heard that voice, and she felt the crippling anxiety clawing into her chest from her belly, and she opened her eyes and gasped.

She stood there.

Holding the rifle.

Shaking.

Looking down the slope.

Past the hanging bodies.

Towards the murmurs of life.

She looked back over her shoulder again.

She tightened her hands around the rifle.

She swallowed a thick lump.

And then she shook her head, and she walked towards that flicker of life.

Somewhere in the distance, from afar, she swore she felt a presence, closing in...

KEIRA

* * *

Keira lay on the floor, Kevin hovering over her with that knife, and she listened to the infected banging and banging against the door...

And as much as she tried to fight it, as much as she tried to resist the fact... she couldn't shake the feeling that time was running out.

It was dark. But bright lights flickered in her eyes, flashed in the way of her vision. She could see Kevin, right above her, holding that knife. He was crying. He was actually crying. And she felt for him. As mad as it sounded, she actually felt for him.

Because she felt like he was being sincere. He was actually being sincere.

He didn't want things to go this way.

He'd just watched his people all turn into infected.

He'd just watched all the people his group had *saved* turning into infected.

And then he'd found out Nisha was bitten. So naturally, quite naturally, he'd just put two and two together. And the conclusion he'd come to was obvious.

Nisha was responsible for this.

She was responsible for what was happening at the bunker.

She was responsible for how everyone had turned.

She was responsible for the violence.

She was responsible for the pain.

She was responsible for all the loss.

And it needed dealing with.

But at the same time... she wished he'd listen to her as she lay there, pinned down on the floor. Head aching. She'd thrown herself in the way of him as he swung the knife towards Nisha. And he'd pushed her to the floor. Pinned her down. Made it hard to breathe. The taste of blood covered her lips. Her ears rang. Her head throbbed with agony.

But she had to stay focused.

She had to stay strong.

Because... the infected.

Banging on the door.

And Nisha.

She'd only just woken up. Only just come round. She was still in danger. She was still weak.

And Rufus. Barking away. Growling. Whining. His sounds echoing around this tiny room they were in. All of it was dizzying. All of it felt like it was on the verge of collapsing. Of falling apart.

"I can make it quick," Kevin begged. "I'm—I'm sorry. For what happened to her. I'm so sorry. But what she's done..."

"She hasn't done this," Keira begged.

"She admitted it!" Kevin shouted. "In the note. She admitted it, Keira. I'm sorry. But you have to see. You just... you just have to see."

And Keira didn't want to see it. She didn't want to accept it. Because accepting it was making it real. Accepting it was accepting the possibility that Kevin was right.

But how could she deny it?

How could she possibly deny it?

Because Nisha *had* written that note.

She *had* written those words.

I've done something bad.

She'd done this.

Somehow... she'd done this.

But it didn't make sense.

None of it made any sense at all.

She knew Nisha was capable of things beyond her understanding.

But *this*...

This just didn't make any sense.

"I know you care about her," Kevin said. "But she's going to turn. Like everyone else."

"She isn't going to turn—"

"And we're trapped in here with her. We're trapped right here with her. So we have to do something. We have to stop her turning. For her own benefit. And for our sakes, too."

Keira shook her head. "Kevin," she said. "She's not infected..."

Another bang.

Another slam at the door.

It sounded like it was going to cave in. Even though it was solid, it sounded like it was going to split right open.

Almost like the infected frenzy outside was growing.

Like they could sense the chaos inside this room.

They could sense the violence.

And they were getting closer and closer.

Kevin looked down at her with bloodshot, tearful eyes. "If you won't let me do what I have to do," he said. "You have to understand. I have... I have to protect myself. Please don't make me do this. Please."

Keira lay there on her back, and she didn't know what else to say. She didn't know what else she could possibly say.

She'd tried bargaining with this guy.

She'd tried convincing him.

But there was nothing else she could do.

There was nothing else she could say.

"Don't make me do this," he said. "Please don't make me do this. Don't..."

And then he stopped.

And Keira didn't understand why. Not at first.

She didn't understand why he'd stopped.

She didn't know what had stopped him.

But something had.

Something. That she couldn't quite put her finger on.

But something... undeniable.

She saw him turn around, and she realised exactly what it was right away.

The infected.

They'd stopped banging on the door.

Everything had gone silent.

Rufus's growling and barking.

Kevin's panting.

But the infected... silent.

Keira's body froze. Everything went numb and silent, just for a second.

The banging.

It'd stopped.

And the groaning had, too.

What was happening?

What was this?

She felt a difference. A subtle difference in the atmosphere. Something she couldn't put her finger on. Something she couldn't quite describe.

But something... there.

Something undeniably there.

She looked up over his shoulder when she saw something that turned her skin cold.

The door.

The door out of this room in the bunker.

It was open.

But it hadn't been barged open.

It was just...

Open.

Like someone had opened it.

And that someone was standing right there.

Right in front of the door.

Rufus stood there. At the back of the room. Tail between his legs. Hackles raised. Growling.

And in front of him...

Nisha.

Nisha stood at the door.

The infected stood outside the door.

Staring right at her.

The door.

Nisha had opened the door.

And the infected were here.

SARAH

* * *

Sarah fell back against the hard garage floor, and pain split through her shattered, broken body.

The darkness filled with light. The light from the outside of this garage she was in. And the light that came from her head slamming against the floor. The hard concrete cracking against her skull. The flash of light filling her eyes as the taste of blood filled her mouth, as she clamped down on her tongue with her teeth. A bitterness in her mouth. Agony coursing right through her bloodstream. Chest tight. Heart pounding. Lying on the floor in agony. In total agony.

And it was all because of this fucker standing over her.

He stood there. The man in the balaclava. The balaclava pulled up over his mouth. His burning eyes, searing above it, the gap revealing some of his face. She could tell he was smiling. She could tell he was enjoying this.

And she could hear other noises outside, too. Behind him. The sound of dogs barking. The sound of people laughing. Hard to tell how many people were here from those sounds. Hard to tell if there were ten. Fifty. A hundred.

But what did it matter?

What would it matter if it were just her and this fucker, standing over her?

She was still down.

She was still on the floor.

There was no getting up.

Up to her feet.

Out of this mess.

The pain in her bleeding, dog-bitten leg.

And the pain splitting its way down her spine and clawing its way into every single corner of her body.

She was fucked.

It didn't matter if there were a hundred people here or if it was just her and this bastard.

She was well and truly fucked.

He stepped into the garage. Dripping rain fell from his dark hood. "I didn't think the bands were tight enough. Figured I'd wait and see. Just to be sure, you know?"

Shit. So this bastard *knew* she might escape. He knew there might be a chance she got away. He'd waited. He'd let her *feel* a moment of hope.

And then, when her hope was at its highest, when she was finally beginning to entertain the possibility of getting away from here, of escaping... he'd pushed her back, and he'd stamped on her wounded leg, and he'd left her there. Lying on the garage floor.

Fucked.

He walked closer to her. Looked down at her. And she noticed something else, then. That baseball bat. In his hand. The nails protruding from its body. Wasn't that a trope of some other post-apocalyptic story she'd seen on television? A villain with a baseball bat in some zombie show? She wasn't entirely sure what she was remembering or imagining right now.

She just knew that she was royally screwed.

He looked down at her. Stared at her, there on the floor. And she felt so weak. She felt so pathetic. She felt so defenceless. So helpless.

Helpless as he stood there, swinging that baseball bat a little from side to side.

Peering down at her.

Smirking.

She felt like she was back in the cupboard again.

She felt like she'd disappointed Dean again.

She felt weak again.

Like the many times she'd felt her own piss seeping through her knickers. How brutally disappointed that made Dean. Because he told her to hold it in. He told her to wait. He told her how disgusting it made her.

But still, he'd keep her there, the smell of urine surrounding her.

Almost as if he was *waiting* for her to urinate.

Waiting for her to slip up.

All for another chance to humiliate her.

All for another chance to punish her.

"You might think you're clever, sugar," the guy said, reaching down and grabbing her face hard with his bony hand. "You might think you're tough."

He squeezed his fingers even tighter around her cheeks. Digging right into her cheekbones.

"But you're not," he said. "You're weak. You're pathetic. And you still haven't realised, have you? You still haven't connected the damned dots."

She gulped. Her mouth was dry. Barely any saliva present.

"If you don't take us to any group. If you don't help us. Then it's game over for you. That's just the way it goes."

She sat there. Burning pain in her bleeding ankle. And right down her spine. Did she tell of Keira? Of Nisha? Of the military men? Maybe two weeks ago, she might've done. Maybe even more recently than that—as much as it pained her to admit.

But now... she was different.

Now, everything was different.

She looked up into the man's eyes, and as terrified as she was, as tempted as she was to comply... as tempted as she was to revert to her old, selfish ways... she knew it wasn't even an option.

"It is what it is," she said.

And then she spat.

Right in his face.

She watched him back off. She watched his eyes widen. She watched that blob of saliva ooze down his face. She watched him wipe it away, look at it with wide, puzzled eyes, and then look back at her. Not saying anything. Not for a moment.

And then he slapped her.

Slapped her with the back of his hand.

Hard.

The taste of blood flooded into her mouth. She felt more pain filling her skull this time. Ringing in her ears.

And then another explosion of pain.

Dean again.

The cupboard again.

All of his punishment, all of his torture, all over again.

And...

No.

No.

She didn't want to think about the last day.

She didn't want to think about the day of the infection.

She didn't want to think about what happened when things went bad.

Or how recently that actually was.

The memory she was trying to suppress.

The *truth* she was trying to suppress.

The man grabbed her. Held her by her hair. Tight.

"I think it's time," he said.

Sarah's stomach sank even further. Her heart raced. Time? Time for what? And did she even want that question answering?

And then, whether she liked it or not, the man answered.

"It's time for us to go on a little walk," he said. "It's time I introduced you to the boys. And it's time we found out what you have to offer us. *Exactly* what you have to offer us."

NISHA

* * *

Nisha opened the door.
But this time, everything didn't turn red. Nothing changed. It was still dark. She was still awake. She didn't feel like she was in a dream. She didn't feel like she was in the bad people's heads. Or their bodies.

She was standing there.

The door was open.

And the bad people were on the other side of it.

Looking right in the door.

Right at her.

They stood there in the dark. She could see them a little bit because there were a couple of candles flickering in the corridor. The bad people looked... sad. Weirdly. A man with grey hair in army clothes. He looked like he was crying. Like he was looking at her and begging her to help him. Like he was sick. Like he just wanted help.

They want you, dear.
They want you.

Only you can help them.

That *FEELING* again, right inside her.

Speaking to her.

Speaking to her from within.

And it was strong. That was the only thing that felt weirder about this than usual.

She could feel that feeling inside her.

She could *HEAR* that voice in her head.

Like someone speaking to her.

Only you can help him only you can help us only you can help all of us—

But then she pushed that voice away.

She pushed that voice away, and she saw their mouths moving wide.

She saw the blood on their teeth.

She saw the flesh dripping from their lips, down their chins.

She saw them, and she smelled them, too.

The wee.

The blood.

The poo.

All of it mixing together, with that soily smell.

She stood there, and she looked right at the man at the front of the bad people. And she didn't feel like she was even trying this time. A bit like the first time she'd stopped them, when Mrs Thompson was attacking her. She didn't have to *do* anything then, either.

She just stood there.

They just stood there, too.

And even though she could feel that voice in her head getting louder, those bad people *wanting* to get closer, and the *FEELING* in her chest *SPEAKING* to her, telling her—

You have to let us in, dear, you can't resist us forever, you are her, you are Mother, you are us, we are you, and—

The girl.

In her head.

The girl in chains.

The girl with tears rolling down her face.

She looked sadder now.

She looked sicker now.

And Nisha needed to tell Keira about this girl.

She needed to get out of here, and Keira needed to get out of here, and Rufus needed to get out of here, and they needed to find this girl.

Because this girl was the only one who could help.

Nisha didn't know how she knew it or if she was going crazy, but she was the only one who could help.

But they had to get out of here first.

She stood there. The bad man stood there. And she didn't even know if Keira was okay. She didn't know what was happening to any of them.

Just that she'd opened the door 'cause the *VOICE* told her to.

But now she didn't want to listen to the voice.

Because the voice was bad—

No not bad we're not bad we're better everything's better with us no more sadness no more war no more pain all united all—

These feelings, like words in her head... she didn't understand them. They didn't make sense. They were just noise. But she *could* understand them as much as she could tell that they were words, and those were the words that had been *SAID*.

But she got the feeling they were bad.

And that she didn't want to listen to them.

Not anymore.

She took a deep breath and turned around and saw Keira and the army man looking back at her.

They both looked at her. With wide eyes.

Then, at the bad people at the door.

Like they were scared.

And Rufus. Poor Rufus looked scared, too.

But Nisha wasn't scared.

Not anymore.

Because Nisha felt...

Strong.

She reached out her hand.

She took Keira's hand.

She helped her to her feet while the man looked on with wide eyes, his mouth moving, his eyes twitching.

She held Keira's shaking hand tight.

And then she looked down at Rufus, and she stroked him.

And then she took a breath.

A deep breath.

And then, like it was the easiest thing in the world... Nisha walked.

The bad people stood there.

They looked at her.

They watched her.

They waited.

And she could feel Keira slowing. Stopping.

But Nisha kept walking.

Because she knew she was safe.

She was okay.

She walked.

Further.

And...

The bad people.

They started to move.

Move out of her way.

Move to the left.

To the right.

And she walked past them.

With Keira.

With Rufus.

With—

Yes you know what you have to do dear. Not ideal not good Mother but for now... for now... we need feeding we need sacrifice we need...

I know, Nisha thought. *And you'll get one.*

She looked back around.

Looked right at the army man.

Looked right into his eyes.

Saw him get up.

Saw him try to leave the room.

And then she looked around at the bad people, and she saw them turning.

Twisting.

Shaking back to life.

Yes, dear, the voice said. *You've done good. For now. Thank you, Mother. Thank you.*

She looked back at the man as he tried to leave the room.

As he tried to get away.

She saw him standing there.

She saw him shaking his head.

She saw him begging.

She saw him pleading.

And then she took a deep breath, holding Keira's hand, and watched them all surround the man.

She watched them all bite him.

Push him to the floor as he fired into the air.

She saw them dig their teeth into his arms.

Into his shoulders.

Into his belly.

Ripping out his insides as blood splattered everywhere.

She saw his mouth widen, a silent scream emerge, as drool trickled down his lips.

PLEASE, she could see him shouting. *PLEASE.*

But it was the other voice she heard louder.

The voice inside her.

The voice that *was* her.

Thank you, my dear.
Thank you.
For now.

She turned around, Keira's hand in hers, Rufus beside her, and they ran down the dark alleyway of the bunker and away from the darkness.

SARAH

* * *

Sarah felt the man in the balaclava drag her by her hair, and as much as she wanted to stand up to him, as much as she wanted to fight, she knew she was in deep, deep shit.

The splitting pain across her tender scalp sent bright lights flickering and racing across her eyes. She let out a cry as the pain intensified. Her heart raced. Her legs were weak, and the pain from the dog bite on her ankle was so strong, so intense. She could taste blood on her lips. She was tired. She was exhausted. She wanted to stand up for herself. She wanted to fight.

But she didn't have any fight left in her.

She could only try to wriggle free of this balaclava-man's grip as he dragged her off the dusty, damp, cold floor of the garage and towards the light of the door.

She tried to pull herself away from him. She tried to escape him. She tried to run. Because she'd been so close to running. She'd been so close to getting away. She'd been so close to escaping.

Or had she?

It might've felt like she was close to getting away. But had she been close, really?

Because he was standing right at that door when she opened it.

Waiting for her.

Almost like that was the plan.

Like it was some sort of trap.

The man dragged her along by her hair. Yanked her further along the dusty floor, towards the bright light of the door. She could hear voices out there. She could hear laughter out there. She could smell burning. And she knew it wasn't good. She knew whatever or wherever she was being taken wasn't good.

Because when was it ever?

When was it ever good news when men were leading you somewhere like this?

Balaclava-wearing, baseball bat-wielding men?

"Come on," he said, laughing a little. "Let's get you out of here. You've got some very good friends of mine to meet. Some very good pals. I want you on your best behaviour for them."

And she felt sick. Crippling nausea stretching right through her body. Because she knew what this was. She knew how this went. She knew which direction it always went in.

He was going to take her outside to his friends. Whoever his friends were.

And they were going to abuse her.

They were going to put her through hell.

He pushed her hard against her back. So hard she almost fell over to her knees. Balancing on her dog-bitten leg was hard. And her head was spinning, and her vision was blurring. She wasn't sure she could even make it so far out these doors before passing out. Maybe passing out would be a blessing right now. Maybe passing out would be the best outcome.

No.

No. She couldn't just lie down.

She couldn't just accept defeat.

She had to stay on her feet.

She had to stay standing.

She had to fight.

She looked up as the man led her out of the garage.

She saw a bunch of dirty old caravans in far worse condition than the one Carly lived in. A couple of VW vans. A campsite, by the looks of things. A campsite in the middle of someone's garden. There were tall gates around the property. Trees everywhere. It looked secluded. It looked cut off. It looked... relatively safe.

But not for her.

Not safe for her by any stretch.

Five men were sitting around a fire in the middle of the garden. A fire, with an old pizza oven beside it. There was some kind of cabin behind them, too. Looked like it might be a converted log store.

But the second the man in the balaclava led Sarah out, they all looked at her.

All of them looked various degrees of sinister. All of them looked varying degrees of mean. She could practically smell the rotten stench of their breath from here. Their dogs—three XL bullies—sat chained to a wooden post in the middle of them, barking away, yanking against that loose post on flimsy-looking rusty chains, making it creak.

The men were eating something. Licking their slimy fingers. Some kind of meat. It smelled strong. It smelled sickly. She didn't even want to think about what it might be. They looked unwell. They stunk of booze—loads of old bottles of whisky and rum sat in front of them, some of them intact, some of them smashed.

But the second they saw her, they all went quiet and all looked at her.

And then at the man behind her.

The man in the balaclava pushed her forward. Towards his group of thugs.

She tried not to think about the way they were looking at her.

The way their eyes searched her.

She tried to maintain her composure. She tried to keep her shit together. This was bad. This was really fucking bad. She couldn't see a way out. All she could see was a group of drunk men with weapons of their own—knives, cricket bats—beside them.

All looking at her like she was a piece of meat.

"Our friend wanted to say hello," the man in the balaclava said. "Where's your manners, boys?"

The man in the balaclava kept pushing her along. And as he pushed her, a couple of the men stood up. Walked up to her. One of them kissed her on the cheek. Another felt her arse, squeezed it tight.

And as she walked on, recoiling physically inside, she started to shiver. That feeling of helplessness. That sense of failure. That sense of inevitability.

The walk towards the inevitable.

The horrible, devastating, inevitable.

Inching closer and closer towards her.

She felt the man with the balaclava grab her shoulder. Felt him hold her there. Stop her walking.

She saw the dogs yanking at their chain leads.

She heard them barking, their barks echoing.

She heard the laughter of the men.

She smelled the flames and the charred meat.

She felt it all filling her body, all of it consuming her, overwhelming her...

And then she felt a hard kick to her ankle, where the dog bit her.

She fell over. Landed on her back. Cracked her head on the ground. Bit her tongue and tasted blood.

But she needed to turn over.

She couldn't just lie here.

She couldn't just accept her fate.

She turned over, and she felt a boot to her right ribcage.

Then one to her chest.

A foot.

Pressing right down.

Right on her sternum.

She looked up and saw the man with the balaclava staring down at her. His balaclava was removed now. In its place, she saw a huge birthmark. A twisted, contorted face. Burns.

"For too long, women like you have looked down on us," he said. "Women like you have turned your noses up at us. You've gone for arseholes and treated us like shit while the good men—men like us—end up getting fucked over by you."

Wait... These fuckers were *incels*? *That's* what this shit was about, at its core? Really?

He pressed his foot harder on her chest.

"We've tried being nice. We tried, back in the old world. But now..."

He lifted that baseball bat.

He pressed it to her head.

Scratched her forehead with one of the long, sharp nails.

"Now, we do things differently," he said.

He looked down at her as his friends spat at her, as they cheered, and as those dogs continued to bark.

He smiled.

And then he pulled back that baseball bat and went to swing it towards her skull.

KEIRA

* * *

Keira looked back at the bunker as the rain fell from above, and she took a deep breath.

It was morning. Or afternoon. Hard to tell. It was bright, anyway. But it was cloudy, too. There was a cool chill in the air, contrasting the stuffiness inside that bunker. The thought of being trapped inside that bunker again filled her with fear. Filled her with dread.

She could only look back at that bunker, at the front of it, and think about the horrors unfolding inside.

Right behind those heavy steel doors.

She gulped. Swallowed the bitter taste of metal. Tasted blood. Her own blood? Infected blood? Hard to tell at this point.

But she was out of the bunker.

Nisha was out of the bunker.

Rufus was out of the bunker.

But there were some things she couldn't stop thinking about.

Some things she couldn't ignore.

Kevin. The military man. Hellbent on making Nisha pay for

what'd happened inside the bunker. The way the infected people had turned.

And Nisha. She hadn't done anything. But... she'd written a note.

A note that suggested she *had* done something.

What had she done?

And how had she done it?

Keira looked down at Nisha. She had her head lowered. A little rain sprinkled down on her from above. It was good to see her on her feet again. It was good to see her *alive* again.

But... there was something about Nisha. An uncertainty. An uncertainty hanging over her. She'd been unconscious for the longest time. She'd seemingly been on death's door. And then she'd woken up, with a terrified note beside her, right by her side.

She looked down at Nisha now. Saw her standing there. The blood caked around her, heavy, purple bags under her eyes. Her shaking, goose-pimpled skin. What did she ask her? And was it wrong that she felt... nervous right now? That she felt... uncomfortable?

Because something had happened down in the bunker.

Deny it as much as she liked. But something had happened.

It was fair to say Nisha's abilities went far, far beyond what she thought.

What she expected.

She could see it on Rufus's face, too. The way he stayed away from her. The way he growled at her. She wouldn't be able to hear it. Nisha wouldn't be able to hear a thing.

But he looked at her, and he growled.

Keira crouched down opposite her. She sat there, shaking for a few seconds. There was so much to fill Nisha in on. And she knew there was only one place she could start, as she stood in the car park of the bunker, still behind the gates, but with Kevin and his people trapped, infected, behind those heavy steel doors.

His screams still echoing around Keira's mind.

Because... Nisha had opened up a path through the infected.

And then she'd turned back and... the way she'd looked at the infected.

The way she'd looked at Kevin.

Keira could be wrong.

But it almost looked as if she had *made* the infected attack Kevin.

Like she'd used him as bait.

She reached into her pocket. For a notepad. But she couldn't find one. She couldn't find anything to write with. She couldn't sign. She was on her own. And Nisha was no doubt confused and lost, and...

Sarah.

On the bridleway.

And...

Dad.

She didn't want to think of Dad.

It still turned her guts to remember what'd happened to him. To remember the way she'd stayed with him as he turned. And then what she'd done *for* him.

The knife.

Into his chest.

Bringing the memories back.

The memories of Blackpool. The lady she'd euthanised.

Of Harriet. The young, bitten girl.

Of...

Mum.

She crouched there, heart racing, jaw quivering, and...

Then she felt a cold hand grab hers.

She opened her eyes.

Saw Nisha looking at her. Staring at her with these wide eyes. These... *dead* eyes.

And she saw something else, then.

In her other hand. A piece of paper. A small, torn piece from that notepad. And a pencil.

She held that piece of paper out to Keira. There wasn't much room to write on it. So she had to be careful. She had to make it count.

When she looked at that piece of paper, her stomach sank.

I'm sorry.

She was sorry. Sorry for what? What had she done? Or just generally sorry for everything that'd happened? It was hard to know. It was impossible to say.

Btu she knew she had to make this paper count.

She took the paper. And the pencil.

And then she deliberated over what to write, what to say.

And then, finally, she knew.

My Dad. Sarah. They're gone. I'm sorry.

She handed it over to Nisha. Tears rolling from her own eyes as the reality of what she'd just written illuminated in her mind.

Dad.

Dad was gone.

So much had happened today that she'd barely even processed it.

Barely even began to accept it.

She saw Nisha's eyes widen just a little as she read it. Then she looked up at Keira. She signed, then. Signed something Keira didn't understand. Then pointed to the word. The word on the page.

Sorry.

Keira gulped. Swallowed a thick lump in her throat.

Okay, she signed. Or at least that's what she thought she'd signed. Nisha had taught her a few basics. And that was one of them. What else could she do? What else could she say?

She looked down at the paper again. Then back at the bunker.

She thought about what she'd witnessed.

She thought about what Nisha had written.

And she saw that space on the note right in front of her, and she took a deep breath.

She took the note from Nisha again.

She held it with shaking hands.

And, without thinking too much about it... she wrote.

She didn't think about what she was writing until she'd finished. Not truly.

But when she looked down at the paper in front of her, when she saw the words staring up at her, she wondered whether she could possibly show it to Nisha. Whether it was fair.

Because she was just a child.

A child she'd been trying to protect.

Right?

She looked down at Nisha and, with a gulp, she handed the paper over to her.

Nisha looked at the words. She studied them. Closely.

And after what felt like forever, she handed it back to Keira with a word at the bottom.

Keira looked down at the paper.

She looked at her own words.

Do you know anything about what happened to Kevin's people in the bunker? Keira had written.

Because... that's what Nisha had admitted herself.

She'd done something.

Something had happened.

Something was different.

Something was changing.

But right beneath those words, those carefully studied words, Keira saw another word.

Just one word.

No.

She looked into Nisha's eyes.

Nisha's dead eyes.

She looked into them, and she wanted to tell her she didn't believe her.

That she thought she was lying.

She wanted to ask her why she was lying.

What secrets she was keeping.

And what was happening inside her mind.

But instead, against all her better instincts... Keira nodded.

She looked at Rufus.

Growling.

Hackles raised.

Then she looked around at the bunker.

Kevin and his people's tomb.

She looked at the gates and at the unknown beyond.

She didn't know where they were going. But a memory hung in her mind.

The North Lancs barracks.

The place Kevin mentioned.

The safe place, out there.

The populated place.

The sanctuary.

That's where they had to go.

That's the only place they *could* go.

She looked back. Out through the gates. Off, over the fields. She thought of Dad. Dad sitting alone in the field.

She thought of what she'd done for him.

She thought of the death she'd given him.

She thought of how tired she was.

How exhausted she was.

And how alone she was.

And then she gulped.

She took a deep breath.

She wasn't alone.

Nisha was right here with her.

And that was her promise.

From day one... that was her promise.

And it was a promise she intended to keep.

A promise that started with the North Lancs barracks.

She didn't know what was next.

But it was just her and Nisha now.

When she turned around, she couldn't shake the feeling that Nisha was watching her.

Closely.

SARAH

* * *

Sarah watched the nail-covered baseball bat swing towards her in slow motion, and she felt her life flashing before her eyes—in all the cliche ways imaginable.

She saw herself on the ground. Lying on her back. A child. Harry crouched over her, stroking her thighs while she lay there, defenceless. She felt herself crying. And she saw *him* crying, too. Crying with fear? Crying with shame? She wasn't sure. She didn't know.

All she knew was how ashamed it made *her* feel.

How that shame had followed her through her life ever since.

And then she was in the cupboard.

Trapped behind those dark doors.

Hearing Dean's footsteps shuffling around outside and wondering just how long it would be before he walked inside the cupboard. Before he opened that door.

And what the hell he might do to her when he stepped inside.

She lay there on the ground in this campsite and felt her back aching. Her neck aching. She felt her body splitting with exhaustion. With pain.

And she watched as this baseball bat hurtled towards her, the man with the balaclava wielding it, his incel friends gathered around him, circling him.

She watched it plough towards his face when suddenly, she heard something from... somewhere in the distance.

Somewhere she couldn't put her finger on.

Somewhere she couldn't place.

But somewhere... close by.

A scream.

The baseball bat stopped.

Right beside her head.

The man in the balaclava looked around.

The rest of his people looked around.

Away from the fire.

Off to their right. Towards the trees.

A moment.

Just a moment.

But long enough.

Sarah looked to her right.

She saw an axe lying there right beside her.

She grabbed it.

And then she swung it at the man in the balaclava's ankle.

Hard.

He let out a splitting cry of pain.

Blood splattered out from his ankle. Oozed out, spurted everywhere, as he screamed.

And a few of the men looked back around at her. Right back at her.

But Sarah wasn't waiting around.

She wasn't lying on the ground.

She wasn't cowering with fear anymore.

She wasn't on the ground beside the wall while Harry touched her legs.

She wasn't in the cupboard, waiting fearfully for Dean.

She was standing up.

She was standing up, and she was holding the axe, and...

She swung it into the chest of the first man who approached her, an old fucker with barely any teeth left.

She heard his ribcage crack and split.

And then she pulled the axe away.

Turned around to another man. Younger. Skinnier. Shaky. Holding a cricket back. Wide-eyed.

She slammed the axe into his throat.

And she didn't hold back.

Because when she swung at that man, as the blood splattered out and spurted everywhere, she saw Harry.

She saw Dean.

She saw all the fuckers who'd stood against her.

She saw all the cunts who had patronised her.

And ground her down.

And abused her.

All her fucking life.

She saw them, and she didn't care that these people weren't infected. She didn't even see them *as* people.

They were monsters.

They were monsters, and they were worse than the fucking infected.

Because the fucking infected weren't in control of their actions, as far as she could tell. The fucking infected weren't in control of this rage.

But these fuckers, these bastards, they had no excuse.

She turned around and saw what the source of the scream was.

Infected.

Drifting into the camp.

Attacking one, two people Sarah hadn't seen before.

Pinning them down and ripping them to pieces.

She saw a man running away.

Holding up his hand.

Piss covering his jeans.

Then tumbling to his knees.

Holding up his shaking hands.

"Please," he begged as Sarah walked up to him. "Please. I never wanted this. I never wanted any of this. Please. Please!"

But Sarah didn't hear his screams.

She didn't hear him begging.

She didn't hear his protestations.

She just swung the axe into his left temple.

Hard.

His skull cracked.

Blood oozed out.

He let out this pitiful gasp.

Like she gasped when Dean beat her in the stomach, kneed her, winded her, and she tried to plead, tried to beg...

She yanked the axe away.

The man fell to the ground.

And she stood there.

She stood there with this axe. Dripping blood onto the ground.

She stood there, and she saw the bodies in front of her.

The bodies of the incel bastards who'd captured her.

Who'd strung those poor women up after putting them through God knows *what* horrors.

She looked around, and she saw the infected. Wrestling with the remaining survivors of this fucked-up camp. So many of them. Appearing through the trees. Out of nowhere.

And then she looked around, and she saw the man with the balaclava dragging himself along.

Bleeding from his ankle.

Dragging himself in the dirt.

He looked around at her.

Wide-eyed.

Shaky.

She tightened her grip on the axe. And as much as she wanted to go over to him, as much as she wanted to finish him herself, as much as she wanted to subject him to the most horrifying of miseries imaginable... she looked up at the approaching infected.

Then she looked back at the man.

She smiled.

And then she turned away.

"No. Help. Please! Bitch. Please!"

She crouched beside him. She grabbed a chunk of flesh and wrapped her long, dirty fingernails around it.

He looked up at her in horror. "What... what are you... argh!"

And then she yanked that chunk of flesh away from his leg.

Dragged it, tore it, sliced at it. Like meat for a stew.

She walked away from the screaming, bleeding incel leader.

She walked over towards the dogs, who yanked at their flimsy rusty chains, barking, saliva dangling from their long, sharp, blood-stained teeth.

She crouched beside them.

She handed the flesh to them.

Watched their eyes widen as they bit it, as they chewed it, as they scrapped for it.

And as they ate, as they indulged... she stroked them.

One by one.

Stroked their rough fur.

"Good lads," she said.

She walked around the back of them, then. Towards the pole they were chained to.

She looked at the leader, lying there, bleeding out from his ankle, screaming.

She looked right into his eyes.

She saw Harry there.

She saw Dean there.

She saw all of them there.

And she smiled.

"Good lads," she said as she raised the axe.

And then she swung it down on the rusty chain.

Snapping it in one.

The dogs burst free.

Ran towards the man.

Towards the screaming leader.

Bits of his flesh dangling from his teeth.

The scent of blood lingering in the air.

She heard his cries as she walked away, axe in hand.

She heard the way he begged.

She heard the way he begged her. In desperation. And in hatred.

And she smiled.

As she walked away, blood smeared all over her, dripping from the axe... she smiled.

And even though Sarah didn't watch... as she walked away, she heard the tearing flesh and the frenzied growls.

And she heard the fucker's screams.

She smiled.

Axe in hand.

She pictured Harry.

She pictured Dean.

She pictured everyone who had wronged her.

And she wasn't on the ground anymore, staring up at the brick wall.

She wasn't hiding in that cupboard, waiting for Dean.

She was on her feet.

She was free.

She took a deep breath of the humid summer air as the dogs savaged their own leader, ripping him to pieces.

She smiled.

And she walked away.

NISHA

* * *

Nisha looked up at Keira as they stood there in the middle of this weird army place, and something inside her felt... different.

It was bright. But it was cloudy. Everything seemed so bright. Like it hurt her eyes to look at the sky. It was probably because she'd been locked away in that army place for so long. It was a weird place. Sort of underground. Like a Teletubby house. She didn't really like the Teletubbies. When she was younger, she always sat in front of the tele and watched the pictures move past, and Dad would always put that on for her. But she wasn't sure about it. She didn't like it. She preferred real stuff. Like nature programs.

Programs where lions chased their prey.

Where they sunk their teeth around the necks of the twitching deer.

She felt like that lion right now.

That feeling. Inside her. Deep inside her. A feeling she couldn't put her finger on. A feeling she couldn't explain. What was it? And where had it come from? It was weird. It felt so... familiar.

And yet it wasn't *her.*

It was... something inside her.

Something else.

Some*one* else.

She looked up at Keira. She could see she was looking at her differently as she stood there, pale. And Rufus, too. He looked at her like he was scared. She could see he was growling at her. And when she looked into his eyes for too long, which he used to be fine with, he looked away and tucked his tail between his legs.

Like he was terrified.

She didn't know what was different. She didn't know what had changed. She didn't know what was wrong.

But something was different.

Something had changed.

Something was wrong.

She looked at Rufus, then back up at Keira, who held on to the note.

She thought about the note. The question Keira had asked.

Do you know anything about what happened to Kevin's people in the bunker?

And she wasn't sure why she lied. Probably for the same reason Keira lied to her about her dad when she first found her. She'd been taught not to lie. Dad always told her lying was bad. Lying was the worst thing.

But this... this didn't feel like a lie that Dad would tell her off for.

She felt like it was a lie she had to tell.

A lie she just had to tell.

She'd said no. But she knew right away that wasn't true. And she even wondered if maybe Keira knew she was lying, too. Because she wasn't stupid. She was clever.

And when Nisha handed her the note and Keira read it... she could see from how her face changed that she didn't believe her.

It was hard to explain. But there was just something about her. Something *different* about her face. About the way she looked up at her. Right into her eyes.

The way she looked at her a bit like Rufus looked at her.

With fear.

She stood there. Looked up at her. And she thought about what'd happened in the bunker. But... but no. She didn't want to think about that. Not again.

She didn't want to feel the pain.

She didn't want to taste the blood.

And she didn't want to *HEAR* the screams...

She thought of something else. David. Keira's dad. And Sarah, too. They were gone. Something had happened, and they were both gone.

Which meant it was just her and Keira and Rufus now.

And how did that make her feel?

She wasn't sure.

Just that she wasn't sure it made her feel... too safe.

Because there was nothing that could make her feel too safe anymore.

She looked back at that army place.

She remembered walking down the corridors in her dreams.

She remembered seeing that man lying in his bed.

She remembered the *WHISPERS* in her head getting louder and louder and louder until she couldn't fight them, she couldn't resist them, she could only ...

OBEY ME.

That voice. The whispers. Again.

A voice.

A voice inside her that felt like a lady's voice. Like a voice, she didn't recognise.

But the more Nisha heard that voice, the more she listened to it... the more she started to think it might be her own voice.

She remembered what she'd done.

On the field. With all the bad people.

The way she'd made them listen to her.

The way she'd made them turn away.

And then she remembered what she'd done inside the bunker, too.

The way she'd travelled into their bodies, one by one.

The way she'd... *INFECTED* them.

All of them.

Infected them with little bats, flying along, flying into their bodies, into their mouths.

And then she remembered standing there and seeing the man with the gun who'd been in a fight with Keira standing at the door with a scared face.

He'd looked at her. Looked right at her.

And she could see him begging.

She could see him shouting.

She could see him pleading with her to let him out with them.

And she told herself he wasn't good. He couldn't be good. Because he'd been fighting with Keira. And nobody good fought with Keira.

But then she realised something.

Something that scared her.

Even if that man *was* good... she would still have left him to the bad people.

Because they needed feeding.

And when *they* were fed... she was beginning to realise something else.

She felt stronger.

She thought of the girl.

The girl in the chains.

Please help me.

Please.

She took a deep breath.

She looked up at Keira. At her fearful eyes.

And then back at the gates of the army place, away from here.

She knew where she had to go.

She knew who she had to find.

But she had no idea what would happen if and when she found her.

She gulped down a bloody lump in her throat.

She felt the *VOICE* inside her.

Screaming at her.

Telling her to keep on going.

And then she swallowed another lump in her throat, and with Keira and Rufus by her side... she walked.

She didn't know where she was going.

But she knew where she had to go.

And every step she took, she could feel that voice deep inside her body.

Deep inside her chest.

Following her every step.

SARAH

* * *

Sarah limped away from the campsite of the incel fuckers and felt a smile stretch across her face.

It was bright. The sun was finally breaking through the thick clouds overhead. It was raining a little. Drizzling. But it wasn't too bad. Wasn't all that bad at all.

She just walked in the light, walked with a smile on her face, and as she walked, as she took deep breaths of that cool, late summer air... she felt like she was free.

For the first time in her entire life, perhaps, she was free.

She didn't know where she was. In the middle of the woods somewhere, sure. Walking into the unknown, absolutely. And she knew it wasn't safe here. She knew it wasn't safe in this woods. She knew there were bad people around. She knew there was a good chance those incel bastards maybe had more people around.

But as she walked away, she couldn't stop thinking about the wild screams that leader in the balaclava made as his own dogs tore him to pieces.

And smiling.

She held the axe in her shaking hand. She was struggling to walk in all truth. Her body was weak. Her dog-bitten ankle was bleeding badly. Every step felt more painful than the last.

And she knew that was trouble. She knew that was bad news. She knew she was going to succumb to the pain eventually. She knew that the pain was going to get so intense eventually that it would debilitate her. That it would put her on the ground.

And she knew that the blood loss from her ankle would floor her eventually. At some stage, it would floor her.

But none of that seemed to matter.

Amazingly, for the first time in her life... none of it seemed to matter at all.

All that seemed to matter?

The fact that she'd made those bastards pay.

The fact that she'd made those *men* pay.

She walked further and further through the woods. She wondered where Keira was. Where Nisha was. Where Rufus was. She wanted to find them. In a sense, it was all she cared about. She didn't want them to fall victim to any of the sort of cruelty she'd witnessed. She wanted them to be okay.

And then there was Carly.

The woman.

The woman in the caravan.

She thought about her and how similar she was to herself, in a way. In ways she didn't want to consider.

In how she'd cut herself off from society.

In how she'd cut herself off from everyone.

But that wasn't Sarah anymore.

Sarah was different now.

She walked through the woods as the pain radiated through her body when suddenly, she heard the footsteps shuffling behind her.

A part of her didn't want to turn around. A part of her didn't want to look. A part of her didn't want to see what she feared she might see.

But she turned around.

Of course, she turned around.

And she saw them.

They weren't running. Which was a pleasant relief. They were staggering. Staggering, exhausted, between the trees.

Infected.

She saw them drifting towards her, three of them, four of them, maybe more. And she stopped. Sighed. Held the axe in her shaking fingers. She could see them approaching. She could see them surrounding her. And again, there was a strange sense of *peace* around her. This bizarre, almost unfamiliar feeling.

A feeling of ease.

A feeling like she'd truly conquered her demons. Banished her demons.

A feeling like she'd stood up to Harry when she lay on the ground, back crippled.

A feeling like she'd stood up to Dean when he'd locked her in that closet.

A feeling like she'd fought back against all of those fuckers, all those years ago, after being pushed down and humiliated again and again and again.

So as those infected approached her, their groans kicked in, and their staggers and stumbles turned to jogs, Sarah didn't feel fear.

She didn't feel any fear at all.

Because she was done being afraid.

She held her axe.

She held it in her crusty, blood-soaked hand.

She watched those infected get closer.

She watched them close in.

She wasn't going to be fearful.

But she was going to fight.

No matter what happened, she was going to fight.

She wasn't a victim.

Not anymore.

And not ever again.

She raised her axe with her shaking hand as she stood there, the infected edging closer.

She watched them hurtle towards her, across the branches, through the trees.

Heard their gasps turn to groans and screams.

"Come on," she said, standing tall. Axe braced. "Bring it on, you fuckers. Bring it on..."

The first of the infected—a bulky blond guy—opened his mouth and threw himself at her.

She took a step back and went to swing, and...

Suddenly, out of nowhere... he stopped.

He stopped.

Froze.

Stared at her.

And he wasn't the only one, either.

The other infected.

They were all stopped, too.

All standing there.

All frozen.

In a way that Sarah had only ever seen with Nisha.

In a way that reminded her of Nisha.

She stood there. Heart racing. What was this? What was happening?

She heard footsteps, then.

Right behind her.

She stared at the dead mass of infected. Frozen. Staring.

And then she turned around.

She saw her.

Standing there.

Standing there and looking right at her.

Blood oozing from her nostrils.

From her ears.

From her eyes.

But reaching up.

Wiping the blood from her nostrils.

Not infected.

Alive.

Very much alive.

But it wasn't Nisha.

It was someone else.

Someone else she recognised.

Carly.

"Come on," Carly said as the infected stood there. Frozen. "There's a lot I need to tell you about. About what I can do. About... about what I've seen. And about... Leonard."

And it was only then that Sarah saw something new about Carly.

Something she'd never noticed before.

Something Carly had kept well hidden before.

Her arms.

Her arms were covered in bandages.

But one of those bandages had come loose.

And in the middle of her left forearm?

A bite mark.

A clear bite mark.

Bitten.

The infected, frozen.

And standing right here before her.

Uninfected.

She was like Nisha.

There were others, just like Nisha.

And Carly was one of them.

THE GIRL

* * *

Emily had spent her whole life in a darkness that she didn't even know was dark.

Because she didn't know any different. When people felt sad for her because she couldn't see, she told them not to because she didn't know any other way. When people described things to her, she imagined them in sound, touch, and smell, and the feeling it sparked inside her.

Emily was just a kid. And she'd spent her whole life in what other people said was *darkness*.

And Emily never knew if she was missing anything. She never really felt like she was missing anything at all.

But when her eyes filled with colour, when all these sparks and flashes filled her head in ways that she couldn't even describe… she knew she was seeing.

And it made her cry.

It made tears stream down her cheeks.

And it made her scared and afraid.

She had been missing out. Her entire life.

But it was all so much to take in right now.

She looked into the darkness that she recognised as darkness now. She didn't know how all this started. Well. She *did*. But she didn't really get it.

It started when Dad ran into her room, panting, and she could feel him shaking, too. And he told her they needed to get away. They needed to run. Because there were bad people outside. Dangerous people.

And he grabbed her and ran out of the room with her. At first, she thought he was playing. At first, she thought it was a joke. She thought it was some kind of game. Dad was good at making exciting games up. He always had been. Whereas Mum preferred watching telly and listening to music, and sometimes Emily would sit with her, let those sounds dance in her eardrums, and fill her head with colour.

But she realised it wasn't a game when she heard the shouts. When she heard the cries. Like animals, like monsters.

But Dad was holding her. Dad was protecting her.

And everything was going to be okay.

Until she felt the sharp pain right across her shoulder.

Her stepmum, who was usually so nice to her. Trisha. So nice to her.

She heard Dad's sadness. She heard his whimpering. And she didn't understand. Not at first. Something had happened. But it was something she couldn't put her finger on. Something she couldn't understand. Not really.

It was only when Dad told her she'd been bitten and might be drifting into a long sleep soon that she realised what'd happened.

She waited. She didn't like sleep. She felt lost in sleep. She had bad dreams that she lost her hearing, too, and that she couldn't hear a thing, and everything was just... empty.

And then she'd wake up choking, coughing, gasping for air.

So she didn't want to fall into a long sleep.

She didn't want that at all.

She waited. Waited in Dad's arms. Waited for so long.

Until... Well, she wasn't sure when things changed, but it was like Dad started to change his mind. He stopped crying. He started saying things like "you're different" and "you're gonna be okay" and "we need to get you to someone who understands."

And that's when Emily realised there was something different about her.

She and Dad walked for a long way. Well. Dad walked, anyway. He carried her. Carried her so far in his arms.

And she heard things. Those nasty screams of the monsters. Only they never seemed to get close to them, and she didn't understand why.

Only... she had this feeling.

This feeling inside her. Getting stronger.

Like those monsters weren't monsters at all.

Like they were just like her.

It was when Dad fell to his knees that she first heard the voice.

The lady's voice. The nice lady's voice. Right there in her head.

She spoke to her.

Don't worry, princess. Everything will be okay. Everything is going to work out. You aren't alone.

And when she heard that voice, she wasn't sure about it at first. She didn't know who it was. What it wanted. Because it kind of felt like it was happening in her head and not in real life. And that made her feel weird.

But...

Something about that voice made her feel comfortable.

Something about that voice made her feel confident.

Something about that voice made her feel like she wasn't alone.

People found them. People, Dad seemed happy to see at first. Military people, he said. A man called Leonard.

Only...

She hadn't seen Dad for ages.

And she was locked up.

Locked up somewhere cold and damp. And she was hungry and thirsty and wondered how long she could go before she passed out completely and went into the long sleep again like Dad worried about.

But then she saw something.

She *saw* something.

She saw the monsters.

She saw so many of them.

More than she'd ever seen before.

All gathering together.

All joining together as one whole thing.

And she realised... she realised that's where the voice came from.

That's who the voice was.

The voice was these monsters.

The voice was *good*.

And these monsters. They weren't bad.

They just wanted to make things better again.

Because *people* were bad.

People caused wars, and people caused suffering and—

Bats.

Flying all around her.

Screeching.

Flapping their wings against her head.

And that's when she first saw The Girl.

She didn't know the girl's name. She was short. She looked Asian. She had beautiful eyes. But she could tell right away something was different about her.

She was deaf.

She looked at the girl, and she could hear the voice in her head.

The voice in her head telling her to bring the girl here, to bring the girl to where she was.

Because they needed to be together.

They were all stronger together.

The girl. She could do things like Emily could do.

She could do things like stop the monsters—no, not monsters, *Angels*.

And she could go into the heads of the Angels.

Just like she could.

There were others, too. Others like her. Others like both of them.

But no one as strong as *this* one.

No one as strong as The Girl.

Yes. She's the one we want here. She's the one who can help us. She's the one who can make us happy, who can bring us together, who can...

She didn't know how she could do it.

She didn't know how it was possible.

How it was real.

But somehow, she was speaking to The Girl.

She was bringing her closer towards her.

She was drawing her closer and closer.

But there was something else, too.

Something else was getting closer.

She didn't know what it was.

But she felt it in the pit of her stomach.

Like fear.

Fear getting closer.

Fear getting stronger.

Every step closer The Girl got to this place... that *fear* got closer too.

That *darkness* got closer, too.

She sat there, shaking, heart racing, and she thought about the bad people here, when suddenly the door creaked open.

She shivered. She went still. Froze.

She sat there.

Heart racing.

She knew who it was.

Who it always was.

Footsteps.

Footsteps echoing closer towards her.

Closer, and closer, and closer.

She sat there, and there was nothing she could do. There was nothing she could say because she was gagged.

And there was nowhere she could go because she was trapped here.

She just sat there.

Listened to the footsteps getting closer.

And then she felt his warm hand on her right leg.

"Hello, dear," the voice said. "It's me. It's Leonard. You don't need to worry. You never need to worry with me."

She felt him close, and she felt the same fear she'd felt when she first saw him.

She felt that same crippling fear surging right through her system.

And she got the feeling that's what he wanted.

That's *exactly* how he wanted her to feel.

"We've got more tests to do, my love," he said. "More experiments. But it'll all be over soon. And you're being so good. So brave."

She thought about the experiments, as he called them.

She thought about how he'd made her stand in the middle of the screaming monsters.

She thought about how he'd made her turn monsters—Angels—against normal people and made them scream.

And she thought about how he'd made her do something else, too.

Something even she didn't know she could do until she tried it.

She made someone change.

She turned someone into an Angel.

Without even touching them... she turned them into a beautiful Angel.

She didn't like the experiments. They made her head ache. They made her taste blood. And they made her sleep for a long, long time.

And they were dark dreams.

They were quiet dreams.

They were horrible dreams of things tugging at her arms and pulling her legs and—

Bats.

"Come on," Leonard said. "Let's get you out of these chains and out of here."

He went to untie her wrist chains.

She felt this fear.

This fear in the pit of her stomach.

But then she took a deep breath, and she smiled.

Because she felt something else, too.

The Girl.

The Girl walking in their direction.

And... that force, following her.

That darkness following her.

Everything was going to be okay.

She followed Leonard, holding his hand, out of the cold room and towards whatever experiment awaited next.

He had no idea.

But she was getting stronger.

And stronger.

She smiled.

And then she stepped out of this room with him.

Holding his hand.

The image of The Girl fresh in her head.

And the image of the dark cloud following her.

Right towards her.

Right towards Leonard's home.
Like Angels.
Beautiful angels.

* * *

END OF BOOK 6

Undead Odyssey, the seventh book in The Infected Chronicles series, is now available.

If you want to be notified when Ryan Casey's next novel is released—and receive an exclusive post apocalyptic novel totally free—sign up for the author newsletter: ryancaseybooks.com/fanclub